"I don't suppose you'd like to sell her."

Logan chuckled. "Charlie and Duster will never be sold."

"How about if I throw in my house? My car? Oh, wait. It doesn't run. Just the house, then. I don't have much else of value."

"Sorry. Not even your house." Laughing, he brushed an errant strand of hair away from Darcy's face. "But you and Emma are welcome to come out anytime to ride them."

"Tomorrow! Can we come tomorrow?" Emma begged. "Please?"

"Probably not, sweetie. But maybe another time."

Emma didn't speak a word on the way home and trudged silently from Logan's truck to the front door.

"Looks like we're going to have a quiet evening," Darcy said as she watched Emma go to the house. "Thanks so much for the wonderful day."

She impulsively gave him a quick hug and stepped back, suddenly feeling a little flustered and awkward at unexpectedly crossing that invisible line between friends and something more.

Yet how could she regret something that felt so right?

A *USA TODAY* bestselling and award-winning author of over thirty-five novels, **Roxanne Rustand** lives in the country with her husband and a menagerie of pets, including three horses, rescue dogs and cats. She has a master's in nutrition and is a clinical dietitian. *RT Book Reviews* nominated her for a Career Achievement Award, two of her books won their annual Reviewers' Choice Award and two others were nominees.

Books by Roxanne Rustand

Love Inspired

Aspen Creek Crossroads

Winter Reunion
Second Chance Dad
The Single Dad's Redemption
An Aspen Creek Christmas
Falling for the Rancher

Rocky Mountain Heirs

The Loner's Thanksgiving Wish

Love Inspired Suspense

Big Sky Secrets

Fatal Burn
End Game
Murder at Granite Falls
Duty to Protect

Visit the Author Profile page at Harlequin.com for more titles.

Falling for the Rancher

Roxanne Rustand

Recycling programs for this product may not exist in your area.

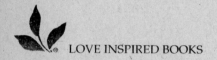

LOVE INSPIRED BOOKS

ISBN-13: 978-0-373-62281-8

Falling for the Rancher

www.Harlequin.com

Printed in U.S.A.

With many thanks to my husband
and our children, for their unfailing support,
and also to the wonderful editors
at Love Inspired who make this all possible.

Love is patient, love is kind. It does not envy,
it does not boast, it is not proud. It does not
dishonor others, it is not self-seeking, it is not
easily angered, it keeps no record of wrongs.
Love does not delight in evil but rejoices in truth.
It always protects, always trusts, always hopes,
always perseveres. Love never fails.
—*1 Corinthians* 13:4–8

Chapter One

After working at the Aspen Creek Veterinary Clinic for the past thirteen months, Dr. Darcy Leighton had encountered a lot of interesting situations. But walking into the clinic on Friday morning to find a tall, dark and muscular cowboy rifling through the file cabinets was certainly a surprise.

It wouldn't be the first time someone had broken in, searching for drugs or money, but this guy looked like he'd never touched an illicit drug in his life. Why on earth was he here, and how had he disabled the new burglar alarm? She and the other staff had inadvertently set it off more times than she could count, to the point that now someone from the alarm company just called her cell to ask if they'd tripped it again.

But there'd been no such call on her cell phone today.

The intruder had tossed an ivory Resistol hat on the desk, and from his pewter fleece vest and long-sleeve shirt to his well-worn jeans and ostrich Western boots, he appeared more suited to a ranch out West than this little resort town in Wisconsin. Not at all like the jittery, tattoo-covered thief she'd inadvertently confronted late one night while returning to check on a surgery case.

"Excuse me," she said sharply, pulling her cell phone from a jacket pocket. She took a single cautious step back and pressed the speed dial numeral for 911. "I think you'd better leave right now, mister. The sheriff will be here any second."

He shot a brief glance at her over his shoulder, then frowned and gave her a much longer second look. With a dismissive shake of his head, he turned back to the files and continued thumbing through them. "Explaining this filing system would be useful. Are you the receptionist?"

Receptionist? Three months ago, the attorney handling Dr. Boyd's estate had sent out a team of accountants who had pored over every last document and computer file for days, then recorded an inventory down to the last paperclip. But this guy sure wasn't wearing a suit and shiny loafers.

"No, I'm not. How did you get in here?"

"A key and the alarm code." He shoved the drawer shut and turned to face her with a sigh. "I'm serious about this filing. Someone here has just a passing acquaintance with the alphabet."

Her gaze landed on the discreet veterinary caduceus logo on the front of his vest. Realization dawned as she stared at a man who had the potential to ruin completely the future she'd so carefully planned. "So…y-you are…"

"The new owner as of last week." He reached forward to shake her hand. "Logan Maxwell."

Still wary, she held back. "We haven't been notified of any sale. Surely the attorney would have let us know."

"That doesn't surprise me. The firm doesn't seem all

that competent." He snagged his billfold from his back jeans pocket, withdrew a business card and tossed it on the receptionist's desk. "Call them."

She swallowed back the knot rising in her throat as she eyed the familiar card with the scales of justice symbol in the center and flowing script, but she went ahead and made the brief call to the attorneys' office anyway. Sure enough, this guy was the new owner. Logan Maxwell, DVM.

The news made her heart sink.

She'd been praying that the practice wouldn't sell until she'd saved enough for a solid down payment and finally found a bank that would grant her a long-term loan. She'd also been praying that if that didn't happen in time, the new owner would want to continue business as usual with her on board.

Maybe a younger version of Dr. Boyd, rest his soul.

Not over six feet of toned cowboy with thick, dark lashes shading startling blue eyes, and a grim, suspicious expression on his way-too-handsome face. What was with that narrow-eyed, penetrating stare, anyway?

He was the one who'd looked like he might be robbing the clinic when she first walked in, while she'd just been coming in to continue working in the career she loved.

She bit back the wave of disappointment settling in her chest with the weight of an anvil as she called to cancel the 911 request. "I'm Darcy Leighton. Dr. Boyd started slowing down, and he needed an associate vet to keep the clinic running."

"So I heard."

She managed a faint rueful smile. "He'd promised

to let me start buying into the practice after I'd been here for a year."

He directed a level look at her. "But according to the attorneys, no contract was ever signed, and no money was paid."

The anvil pressing down on her heart grew heavier, obliterating her long-held dreams. It took her a moment to respond. "Correct. He died six months after I started, but the attorneys wanted the practice kept running until it could be sold, to maintain its value. So we're all still here."

He glanced at the clock on the wall. "Do the other employees come in by seven thirty?"

Darcy nodded.

He tipped his head toward the hallway leading from the waiting room to the lab, two exam rooms, the surgery room and two offices. "Instead of standing here, let's go back to Boyd's office. We have a few things to discuss."

He stepped aside and followed her to the back office, where she hesitated for a split second before dropping into one of the leather club chairs facing the massive old mahogany desk. He settled behind the desk as if it had been his for decades, and she felt a flare of sorrow.

"It doesn't seem right, seeing someone else in his chair. Doc was an institution here in town for more years than anyone can remember."

"And probably well loved, though from what I see in this clinic, he was behind the times."

"He was a good vet," she shot back, defending her old boss though she knew Maxwell was right. "Even if…some of the equipment here is out of date."

The man had the audacity to roll his eyes. "Show me

something that isn't. The list is staggering, but I knew that before buying the place."

She looked at him in surprise. "When were you here?"

"Over a month ago, on a Sunday. I flew in from Montana, and two of the attorneys from Madison met me here. Then I went back to their office and spent a couple days going through the clinic's old financial records."

That explained why she hadn't seen him, then. He'd chosen to delve into the situation when the clinic was closed. "So you've seen that, despite a lack of the latest technology, this practice is busy."

"I hope it continues to be. The horse population in this county is growing rapidly, and there's a real need for an equine practice around here."

"Just equine?" she asked faintly. "What about our small-animal clients?"

A brief grin lifted a corner of his mouth, and she felt momentarily dazzled by the flash of a deep, slashing dimple in his left cheek. If he ever offered a genuine smile, the clinic's circuits just might blow.

"That's all I do, ma'am. Horses."

"Then that's perfect," she exclaimed with a rush of relief. "If you want to focus on horses, I can handle everything else. You've already got an excellent vet tech and receptionist in place."

His gaze veered to the wall of bookshelves. "Actually," he said carefully, as if walking cautiously through a minefield, "I want to have a fresh start. So—"

At a sharp, indrawn breath, he and Darcy looked at the open doorway, where Kaycee, the vet tech, now stood with a hand at her mouth and tears welling in her eyes. Marilyn, the office manager, stood behind her, her face pale with obvious shock.

"You're already firing us—without even giving us a chance?" Kaycee's voice trembled with outrage. "Is that fair?"

"I didn't say that," he said mildly.

"Y-you have no idea how hard we work or how dedicated we are," she retorted. "Doc Boyd always said—"

"Kaycee," Darcy said quietly, though she knew how much the girl needed her job. At just twenty-three, she was supporting her younger brother and sister, while Marilyn had a disabled husband at home.

Knowing their difficult situations, Dr. Boyd had given both of them generous annual raises. There wasn't another job in town that would pay either of them as much for their specialized skills. This practice was the only one for forty miles.

But starting an argument on the new owner's first day wouldn't help anyone's cause.

Darcy looked up at Marilyn. "Are my first clients here?"

The receptionist nodded stiffly.

"Then please get them settled in the exam rooms, Kaycee. I'll be out in a minute." Darcy stood to shut the office door quietly and turned back to the desk with a frown. "They're excellent employees. I can promise you that. I've worked with them for a year. They're both highly professional."

He drummed his long, tanned fingers on the desk. "As I started to say, I feel it's important to have a fresh start here. This is going to be an equine clinic in the future, with far less—if any—small-animal. So I have to assess the kind of staff I really need. And honestly…"

His voice trailed off as he seemed to consider his words, but at the regret and sympathy in his eyes, Darcy suddenly knew exactly what he was going to say. This wasn't just about Marilyn and Kaycee. It was also about her. And given the muscle ticking along the side of his jaw, those changes weren't going to be in the distant future.

What was he going to do—boot her out the door right now? Would he be that callous?

After all she and her little girl had been through during the past two years, she'd thought they were finally secure in their new lives here in Aspen Creek.

Even two weeks' notice wouldn't be enough to get her finances and her future in order. What if she needed to leave town to find employment? How would Emma handle yet another wrenching change?

Blindsided, Darcy felt her heart falter as her thoughts raced through a dozen possibilities. "Even if you're developing an equine practice, you'll find the small-animal side busy and well worth keeping."

"I'm sorry. That's not part of my plan," he said gently.

Time. She needed much more time, and it didn't sound like she was going to get it.

"But it's still going to take a while for you to get up to speed and build up a different clientele, and in the meantime, it sure couldn't hurt to enjoy a solid income." She said a silent prayer and took a steadying breath as she considered just how far she could push him.

"I'll stay on for just the next two months," she continued firmly. "So you can get your feet on the ground here. I'll take care of the clinic appointments while you get settled in and start your horse practice, and then we can reassess. If you realize it's worth keeping the small-animal side going, we can discuss my salary and contract. If not, no hard feelings. I'll just start my own large and small-animal mixed practice here in town. A little competition never hurt anyone, right?"

He stared at her reluctantly for a long moment, then laughed—probably at her sheer audacity—and accepted her handshake. "I guess we have a deal."

A few hours later, Logan settled into a booth at a cafe at the far end of town and sighed heavily. His goal had been simple and should have been easily met, but his first morning at the clinic certainly hadn't gone as well as he'd planned.

Finding the right veterinary practice to buy had occupied his thoughts for months. Finding one within a reasonable distance to horse breeding farms and also the active horse show circuits in Wisconsin and Minnesota had been high on his list.

The Aspen Creek Vet Clinic and associated property had ticked every box. It had once been a mixed practice, so it included a good clinic building with a corral and small stable out back, which made it perfect for conversion into an equine practice. And a few miles out in the country, Dr. Boyd's house sat on twenty fenced acres with another stable. The house and all of the buildings needed updating, but at least he hadn't needed to hunt for a place to live.

The fact that this little Wisconsin town was far from Montana made it even better.

But all of those thoughts about the property and his future here had instantly fled the moment he'd come face-to-face with Darcy Leighton this morning. Warning bells had clanged in his head. His jaw had almost dropped to the floor. He'd had to force himself to stand his ground.

Curvy, with brown hair and sparkling hazel eyes, she could easily have been the much prettier sister of his former fiancée back in Montana, though for just a moment he'd imagined he was staring into Cathy's deceitful eyes and his stomach had plummeted.

His business plan aside, seeing Darcy on a day-to-day basis would be an intolerable reminder of the past. A time when a pretty face and calculated charm had blinded him to clues so obvious that in retrospect he could not believe his stupidity. Two months. He could manage two months. *Maybe*.

Why hadn't he just said no, offered Darcy a nice severance bonus and sent her on her way? And what on earth was that rush of sensation when he'd accepted her handshake? He'd felt his arm tingle and his blood warm, and when his eyes locked on hers he couldn't look away.

It was only when she'd smiled a little and stepped back that he realized he'd held her hand a little too long.

He certainly hadn't felt this instant connection with Cathy…which made those warning bells clang all over again. He could not afford a second mistake.

He ordered a cheeseburger and Coke when the waitress—Marge, given the name embroidered on her uniform—stopped by his booth. Then he pensively stared out the large plate glass window overlooking Aspen Creek's Main Street.

For a chilly Monday morning in mid-April, there was a surprising amount of activity in town. Most of the parking spaces were filled. Pedestrians were window-shopping as they passed the various boutiques and upscale shops probably meant to lure tourists from Minneapolis-St. Paul and Chicago.

Farther down the street, he'd spied some high-end outfitters displaying kayaks, canoes and pricey backpacks in their windows. A quaint two-story bookstore. Cozy-looking tea shops. Bed-and-breakfast signs in front of grand old Victorians.

The town hardly looked like it could be in horse country, but his research had proved otherwise, and so he had started making his plans. Remodeling. Equipment purchases. Supplies. Promotion, to let horse owners know about him.

Under Dr. Boyd's ownership the clinic had been focused on small animals, so he'd figured he would let the current staff go and then hire people with the equine expertise he needed. People he would carefully interview, and then he'd follow up with background checks on. Thorough background checks.

He felt a shudder work down his spine, wishing with every beat of his heart that there'd been more careful scrutiny of staff at the multi-vet clinic where he'd worked back in Montana. But that was over, done with, and now he had a chance to start his own clinic and do things right.

The waitress returned, gave him a narrow look and set his Coke down with a thud. A few drops splattered onto the table, but she wheeled around for the kitchen without a second look.

Curious, he watched her go and realized that every eye in the place was fixed on him. None of them looked friendly. Feeling as if he'd slipped into some sort of time warp, he eyed the Coke but didn't try it.

A stooped, gray-haired man in a bright plaid shirt,

khakis and purple tennis shoes appeared next to his booth. "I figure you must be the new vet," he muttered. He leaned closer to peer at the veterinary emblem on Logan's vest. "Yep. Figured so. Lucky man, buying Doc Boyd's place. He was the best. Best gals working for him, too. Couldn't find any better. You can count your blessings, sonny."

He stalked away, muttering under his breath.

Three elderly women seated at a round table a dozen feet away craned their necks to watch the old guy leave. As one, their heads swiveled toward Logan. If glares could kill, he'd have been turning cold on the floor. Still, he nodded and smiled back at them. "Ladies."

The oldest one harrumphed and turned away. The one with short silver hair fixed him with her beady eyes. "Paul is right. Everyone loved Dr. Boyd, you know. He wouldn't *ever* have treated his staff badly."

"People care about each other in a small town." The third woman lifted her chin with a haughty sniff.

He politely tipped his head in acknowledgment, then startled a bit when a thirtysomething woman slipped into his booth and propped her folded hands on the table.

Judging from the blinding sparkles on her wedding ring, she surely hadn't stopped by to flirt, and given the decidedly unfriendly mood in the café, he hoped she didn't plan to whack him with her heavy leather purse.

"Beth Stone. I own the bookstore in town," she said briskly. "It looked like you might need a bodyguard, so I figured I'd stop by for a minute. Thought I might need to warn you."

He glanced at the other customers in the café, who

were all pushing eighty if they were a day. "I think I can handle them. At least, so far."

Her long chestnut hair swung against her cheek as she slowly shook her head. "Your business affairs are your own, of course. I don't mean to pry, and whatever you decide to do is totally up to you. But as you can see, word spreads fast in a small town. Gossip is a bad thing, but people really do care about each other here, just as Mabel told you. No one wants to see a friend hurt."

Clearly eavesdropping from her seat at the round table, Mabel gave him a smug smile.

"I just wanted to offer a little friendly advice," Beth continued. "If you can, take things a bit slow. Settle in. Get to know people. And if you're going to fire everyone at the vet clinic right off the bat—"

"I haven't," Logan said quietly. *Yet.*

"But that's the word on the street, as they say. Not because your employees are blasting the news all over town," Beth added quickly. "There might have been… uh…a client who overheard something while in the waiting room…who happened to stop here at the café, where no secret is ever kept. Ever."

The waitress scuttled up to the booth and delivered his hamburger, then fled back to the kitchen. "Sounds like my hometown in Montana," Logan said.

"Businesses have failed here over far less, and you don't want to drive every last client to some other vet practice in the next town. Just be prepared."

"Thanks."

"People *care* about each other here. And they are as friendly as can be."

He eyed the other customers in the café, who definitely didn't appear friendly at all. "I'll have to take your word on that."

"I promise you, this really is a wonderful town. There are all sorts of seasonal celebrations that draw crowds of tourists. And I can't think of anyone who doesn't have at least one pet, so you'll be plenty busy." She gathered her purse and stood. "And I know you'll really like the staff at the clinic when you get to know them. I've been taking our pets there all of my adult life, and they provide excellent care."

"Good to hear." He poked at his hamburger, which appeared to be very well done, and cold to boot.

"Dr. Leighton in particular—did you know she completed some sort of special residency after vet school? I don't recall, exactly. Surgery, maybe. Or was it medicine? I know that she received some pretty big honors. There was an article on her in the local newspaper when she first came to town. Dr. Boyd was really thrilled when he was able to hire her."

So here was yet another pitch, though delivered more skillfully than most. "I'll be sure to ask her about it."

Beth nodded with satisfaction. "I've got to get back to my store, but it's been nice to meet you. God bless."

He waited until she left, then cautiously lifted the top bun on the burger. Though nothing unexpected appeared inside, the patty was charred to the point of being inedible—yet another message from the good people of Aspen Creek.

So maybe it was for the best that Darcy had railroaded him into keeping her on for a few months, he realized with chagrin.

He could now become acquainted around town, try to avoid alienating any more of the residents and thus improve the chances that his vet practice would succeed. With a new clinic website, a Facebook page and announcements in the regional horse magazines, word would spread, and maybe he could start his life over again, away from the shadow of his past.

All he needed was time.

Chapter Two

After the Easter service at the Aspen Creek Community Church, Darcy drove up the long lane winding through a heavy pine forest to Dr. Boyd's house, knowing this was probably a big mistake.

Logan certainly hadn't been friendly when he'd first arrived at the clinic on Friday. He'd been gruff and completely lacking in empathy toward her and the clinic staff. He was clearly looking forward to firing them all.

And he probably wouldn't accept her invitation anyway. So why had she even bothered to come?

Because, she muttered under her breath, she should treat him as kindly as she would any other newcomer, even if she had yet to find anything likable about him whatsoever.

"What, Mommy?" Emma chirped from her new booster seat in back.

"Just talking to myself, sweetie." Darcy's mood brightened. Maybe Logan had a wife and kids, and they were all celebrating Easter by themselves, though something about him made her guess that he was probably alone. That would be no surprise, if he was cold to everyone.

She looked up at Emma in the rearview mirror. "I'm guessing that Dr. Maxwell might not want to join us for dinner, but we'll see."

Emma sat up a little straighter to look around and squealed with delight at her surroundings as the house and barn came into view. "Will Barney be here?"

I wish. I wish everything was still the same—that the old sheepdog would come romping out of the barn to meet us, and that Dr. Boyd would be here, too.

He'd been more than a mentor during the seven months she'd worked with him. He'd been kind and perceptive and caring, like the grandfathers she'd never known but had pictured. He'd helped her get through the bleakest time of her life.

But now he was gone, and nothing would ever be the same again.

"Barney lives with Marilyn now, sweetie. Remember? And Dr. Boyd is up in heaven."

"Can we go see Barney?" Emma asked somberly.

"Of course we can. Maybe tomorrow." Darcy pulled to a stop in front of the sprawling, rustic log home with river rock pillars and rock siding at the front porch. Set in the shade of towering pines, the house blended into its surroundings and matched the hip-roofed barn and wood-fenced corrals.

It had been the home of her dreams, but the house and clinic had been far beyond her financial reach.

A gleaming black crew cab Dodge pickup with Montana plates was parked in front of the garage, so apparently Logan was home. She stepped out of her SUV,

smoothed her peach linen skirt and helped Emma out
of her booster seat.

Twisting a strand of her blond hair around her finger, the four-year-old frowned and looked around. "Will
there be Easter baskets here?"

"At home," Darcy promised. She bent down to fluff
the layers of pink ruffles cascading from the waist of
her daughter's dress. "We won't be here long."

A spiral-sliced ham was waiting in the oven back at
the cottage, and creamy mashed potatoes were staying warm in a Crock-Pot. Several colorful salads were
finished and in the fridge. But the day seemed strange
again this year, with just the two of them to celebrate
the joy of Easter.

It had to be different for Logan, as well, assuming he
had observed the usual Easter traditions back in Montana. Then again, was he even a believer? Beyond the
fact that he'd arrived intending to fire her, she knew
nothing about him.

At the sound of hammering out past the barn, she
took Emma's hand and headed that way, taking in the
contrast of the many new boards that now replaced the
broken ones.

As they rounded the barn, he came into view. He
eyed the three-plank oak fence line stretching toward
the heavy timber to the west. Tapped a top board upward into perfect alignment and nailed it in place.

"Hello there," Darcy called out. "Happy Easter."

He spun around, clearly startled, and frowned as he
dropped the hammer into a loop on his low-slung tool
belt. He gave them a short nod.

It wasn't much of a greeting, but she resolutely strode

forward with Emma in tow. "Looks like you've been working hard since you got here."

"Yesterday and today." He tipped his head toward the corral. "I need at least one safe corral finished before I can go back for my horses and the rest of my things."

Emma had shyly hung back behind Darcy, but now she took a tentative step forward. "You have horses?"

His cool demeanor softened as he looked down at her. "Just two. Drifter is a pretty palomino mare just about the color of your hair, and Charlie is a bay gelding with four white socks and a blaze. I've had him since I was twelve."

She looked up at him in awe. "I want a pony but Mommy says not 'til I'm bigger. That's too long."

Darcy cleared her throat, knowing all too well where *that* conversation was heading. "We actually stopped by because I figured you don't know anyone in town yet, and thought you might like to join us for Easter dinner this afternoon. I didn't think to ask you when we first met on Friday."

"Well, I…"

"It's just the two of us here in town, so we won't have a big family gathering or anything."

Emma's eyes sparkled. "Could you bring a horse?"

He looked down at her and chuckled. "That would be fun, but I'm heading back to Montana as soon as I put away my tools."

Emma's face fell. "Mommy even made my favorite pink fluffy Jell-O. And then I get to hunt for Easter baskets. What if there's one for you?"

That deep slash of a dimple appeared when he smiled at her. "I think I'm too old for that, darlin'. But I know you'll have a great time."

"We'd better go home and let Dr. Maxwell finish up so he can get on his way." Darcy reached for her hand. "I hope you have a safe trip. Let Marilyn know when you'll be back, in case someone asks."

When he looked up at Darcy, his warmth faded as quickly as if he'd turned it off with a switch, and he was back to his aloof business persona. "Probably Thursday or Friday."

"Uh...I'll let her know. Safe travels." She turned away and headed back to the car with Emma.

How awkward was that? He'd shown kindness to Emma, but if he was this cool and distant with his clients, he wasn't going to fare well.

Though if he didn't connect well with them, maybe he'd eventually put the practice up for sale, and perhaps by then she'd be able to find favorable financing. A little flare of hope settled in her heart.

Maybe her dreams could still come true.

"We're down to only fourteen volunteers now," Beth said on Friday afternoon as she studied the list on her iPad. She drummed her fingers on the vet clinic receptionist's counter. "I never expected six would cancel. All of our posters promised there would be twenty, and the handyman fundraiser auction is tonight. Guess I was too optimistic."

"There should still be enough money for the church youth group trip, though," Darcy said.

"For the kids, probably. But not enough to cover the chaperones' expenses, and some of those parents just can't afford it otherwise. Without enough chaperones, the trip is off. Have you asked Logan to participate? I'll bet he would be willing."

"Ask him? I barely know him." Darcy shuddered. "He doesn't seem like the benevolent type. And this would be an awfully big favor."

"Wouldn't it be a great introduction for him in the community, though? Participating for such a good cause would surely cast him in a more favorable light. He didn't exactly have an auspicious start in town."

"Thanks to Paul Miller, who had no business starting those rumors at the cafe." And mostly thanks to Logan himself, but she tried to rein in that uncharitable thought. "For all I know, Logan doesn't even have the skills for this sort of thing. I've seen him wield a hammer, but that was only on a fence board."

"Call him and find out," Beth insisted. "You have his cell number, right? Tell him the auction is for just twenty hours of labor. Surely he could manage to do something useful for someone."

"Maybe. But I haven't even seen him all week—not since he showed up and announced that my career, my whole life, is being turned upside down. Marilyn's and Kaycee's, too, and you know how much they need their jobs." Darcy thought for a minute. "Oh, and I also saw him briefly last Sunday, when he refused my invitation for Easter dinner and was pretty much cold as ice when we talked. A very brief conversation, I might add."

Beth grinned. "And here I thought he might just be the perfect match for you. Handsome, same career, lots to talk about…"

Darcy snorted. "No way. Sounds like fairy-tale stuff to me. Been there, done that, and I'm not going down *that* road again. Ever."

"If he's been gone all week, maybe he's changed his

mind about buying the clinic and is scouting out other possibilities."

"I wish," Darcy retorted dryly. "But I think the purchase of the clinic is a done deal. Signed contracts and all of that. He called the clinic this morning and told Marilyn he'd be back sometime late today with his two horses and the rest of his things. That sounds permanent to me."

"So, will you make that call?" Beth fixed Darcy with an expectant look. "Please? We could bend the rules so he wouldn't even need to appear onstage."

Darcy laughed, remembering Logan's narrow-eyed glower when they'd first run into each other at the clinic. "That actually might be for the best no matter when he shows up back in town."

"Just be sure to let my assistant know as soon as you have an answer, because Janet will be printing the final version of the program at six thirty, and the auction starts at eight."

There were reasons Beth had made such a success of her bookstore, and sheer determination topped the list. Darcy sighed heavily as she glanced at the clock on the wall. "I'll send him a text. I need to take Emma to her dental appointment at four, and I'll be busy with clients all afternoon. If he doesn't respond by then, Kaycee can ask him when he stops in."

Beth beamed. "Perfect."

"Well, hang on to that thought, but I doubt he'll agree. Anyway, I suspect most bidders have already set their sights on the handyman they prefer, so Logan might not generate much for the fundraiser."

"Are you still planning to bid on Edgar Larson?"

"Absolutely." Darcy fervently clapped a hand against her upper chest. "He is the man of my dreams."

Beth laughed. "But just a bit old for you, sweetie— by forty years at least. And don't forget about Agnes."

"All the better. I understand Ed is the best craftsman in the bunch, and my late aunt's cottage is in serious need of repairs. And I hear his wife sends along her incredible caramel rolls whenever he starts a new job."

"So I've heard. Those rolls alone should double his worth during the bidding."

"I sure hope not. But I suspect every single, divorced or widowed woman in town wants to win him as much as I do."

"As do all of the women whose husbands can barely change a lightbulb. Edgar is our biggest draw every year, bless his heart. Last year he was first on the program, and a third of the audience left as soon as his work was auctioned. This year, we've got him last."

"I'll sure be hoping. Last month I did a lot of calling around, trying to find someone to start doing repairs and updating. The reputable firms are booked at least six months out, and I may no longer have that kind of time to wait."

Beth rested a comforting hand over Darcy's. "Our whole book club is praying you'll be able to stay in town one way or another, believe me."

"I'm praying, too. But I still need to be prepared." Darcy tapped a brief text to Logan and held up her phone for Beth to see, then hit Send. "There, it's done."

"Thanks a million." Beth leaned in for a quick hug. "Now we're all set."

Probably not, Darcy thought as she headed into an exam room, where a cocker spaniel was awaiting a health exam and vaccinations. Would Logan even consider the request?

There was no answer to her text by the time she'd finished with the spaniel.

Nothing by the time she finished with her other appointments and gathered her purse and car keys to go pick up Emma. Of course not. She hadn't expected him to agree, but at least he could've been thoughtful enough to respond.

She stopped in the kennel room, where Kaycee was checking on the IV running for a beagle recovering from surgery. "I still haven't heard back from Dr. Maxwell. Can you keep trying to reach him? Or tell him about the auction if he stops by the clinic?"

"No problem."

"Oh, and let Janet or Beth know about his answer, in case they need to add his name to the program."

"Will do." Kaycee shut the cage door, turned around and grinned. "Did I hear you say that you're pinning your hopes on Edgar? He's my uncle, you know. Crotchety as can be."

"So I hear, but I'm praying he'll agree to continue working for me after the twenty hours are up."

"Best wishes on the bidding, 'cause it's probably your only chance of getting him to do any work for you. Outside of the annual youth group auction, he's superfussy about who he works for. Says he's semiretired."

"So…if I don't have the winning bid, you could put in a good word for me later on?" Darcy said. "Please?"

"I'll ask, but it probably won't make any difference. His own niece tried to hire him for a project last winter and he flat-out said no. Then again, the whole family knows she's high-maintenance, and he probably didn't want the bother."

"I promise you that I'm not," Darcy said with a smile as she headed for the door. "I'm desperate, not difficult."

As she drove to the babysitter's home to pick up Emma, the truth of her own words weighed heavily on her heart.

The cottage needed a lot of work, as dear old Aunt Tina hadn't been able to keep up with repairs and updates during her final years. But now there was a ticking clock to consider.

If Logan Maxwell did let her go at the end of two months, her options would be to establish a new practice here—a financial impossibility right now—or to find a practice elsewhere, looking for an associate. But how would the cottage ever pass the mortgage home inspection for a buyer if she suddenly had to sell it and move on?

As she waited at the only stoplight on Main Street, she looked heavenward and briefly closed her eyes. *Please Lord, help me win the bidding for Edgar—and give me more time to work things out.*

A large crowd had already gathered in the church reception hall when Darcy arrived with Emma in tow just minutes before Pastor Mark began his opening remarks at a podium.

Two long bake sale tables displayed delectable treats, while several other tables offered arts and crafts items. At the far end of the room, two women were offering hot chocolate and coffee from the kitchen serving window.

"I know you just had supper at home, but would you

like some hot chocolate or a treat?" Darcy asked. "I see some pretty frosted cookies on that table."

Emma nodded somberly. "A cookie. Can we go home?"

"Um...I need to stay, sweetie." The daytime baby-sitter who took care of Emma after morning preschool every day was rarely available for evenings, and Darcy hadn't been able to find anyone else.

She settled Emma on a chair with her cookie and took the chair next to her. "One of the nursery ladies and some teenagers from the youth group are watching kids in the nursery. Would you like to go play with them?"

"I wanna go *home*."

Emma's mood didn't bode well for the evening, but Darcy could hardly blame her. It had already been a long day for her, and this was now Emma's usual bath time, to be followed by a bedtime snack and a stack of books to read. In the hope that Edgar had been moved to an earlier time slot, Darcy opened her program and looked down the list.

It was up to fifteen names now, each followed by a brief description of the types of handyman jobs they preferred. Some were members of the church with other careers but willing to mow, rake or help paint. A few offered to help with household repairs or a specific auto maintenance task rather than the twenty hours. A couple said "negotiable."

Edgar was still at the end of the list and... Oh, my. Darcy drew a sharp breath in surprise. There was Dr. Logan Maxwell's name, second to last. No skills listed. She glanced at it again in disbelief. He'd actually volunteered?

Surprised, she glanced around the crowded room

trying to find Beth or Janet…or even Kaycee, who had planned to take a shift at the bake sale table. Glimpsing Kaycee in the crowd milling at the back of the room, she dropped her jacket on her chair. "I'll be right back, sweetie. You'll be able to see me just right over there."

Emma looked up from nibbling the edge of her cookie and yawned. "Then can we go home?"

"In a little while. Once it gets started, the auction shouldn't take long." She strode toward the crowd as Pastor Mark yielded the microphone to Lewis Thomas, a short, spare man with thinning hair and a booming voice, who encouraged vigorous bidding for the sake of the youth group, then began describing the terms of the auction.

He abruptly launched into a rapid-fire auctioneer's patter, and one after another, the handyman volunteers were auctioned off. Fifty dollars. A hundred. Several went for one fifty.

A woman with a gleam in her eye shouted, "One seventy-five! That one's my husband, and now he'll *have* to take care of my honey-do list!"

The audience erupted in laughter.

"Hey, Kaycee," Darcy called out as she edged through the people pressing forward toward the podium and made her way to Kaycee's side. "I'm dying to know what Dr. Maxwell said—and how you convinced him to volunteer. Will he be here tonight?"

A faint blush bloomed on Kaycee's cheeks. "I'm really sorry, Doc. I never saw him at the clinic. I left two messages on his cell, but he never called back."

Darcy felt the blood drain from her face. "B-but he's on the program."

The younger woman's eyes widened. "Maybe he talked to someone else?"

"He wouldn't have known anyone else on the committee." Darcy bit her lower lip. "I'll find Beth or Janet. No worries."

"If he's listed and his work commitment is auctioned, he's *got* to follow through, it's like a *contract*," Kaycee said darkly.

"Surely not if the listing is a mistake," Darcy retorted. "Try calling him right now. Find out if he knew about this and get him over here right away. He doesn't need any more bad press in town. I'll try to find Janet and get his name removed."

But as she turned to scan the crowd, her gaze landed on Emma. The little girl was still dutifully sitting in her chair a dozen feet away, the cookie barely touched, and tears were trailing down her cheeks. Darcy's heart lurched as she hurried over, slipped into the chair next to Emma's and gave her a hug. "I'm so sorry, honey— but you did see where I was, right?"

Emma gave an almost imperceptible nod.

"And did you see your Sunday school teacher just over there? And you know Beth, and Sophie—" Darcy glanced around. "I even see Hannah in the next row. You were safe, I promise."

Emma nodded tearfully, her lower lip trembling.

"Stay right with me while I find someone, all right?" Darcy scooped the child up into her arms, and Emma sagged against her shoulder, too tired to answer.

Darcy tried to make her way through the crowd, but now everyone was out of their chairs, craning their necks to see who was up next as another five handyman volunteers were auctioned in quick succession.

"Dr. Logan Maxwell," the auctioneer shouted above the hubbub. "New guy in town, and already helping the community. Gotta give the guy credit. Doesn't say what kind of work he can do, but let's go. Starting at two hundred, folks—who is ready to go?"

Darcy froze in horror as the auctioneer's voice slipped into an almost indecipherable sales patter and the crowd fell silent.

People exchanged glances.

A few snickered.

A stage whisper filtered through the room.

"Who'd want to bid for the likes of him? My poor cousin works at the clinic and said she'd soon be out on her ear…"

Time seemed to stop as more whispers spread through the room. Then the room fell silent once again when the auctioneer dropped the starting bid to a hundred seventy-five. A hundred fifty. "C'mon folks…he's a real bargain at that. You'll be helping the kids, and maybe he can even spay your cat."

Uneasy laughter rippled through the audience. "How 'bout a hundred twenty-five, then…"

Darcy desperately scanned the crowd. Surely someone would be glad to grab such a bargain…or maybe just have mercy on him. Right now he was like an outcast, a pariah who would be the talk around town for a long, long time. And from the hard expressions she saw, that wasn't going to change. *Please, Lord, encourage someone to bid.*

Kaycee appeared at Darcy's side. "This is awful. But on the other hand, he's mean and he kinda deserves it."

"No one ever deserves ridicule, and that's what will

happen," Darcy said quietly. "He'll be the only guy who failed to receive a single bid. Ever."

"He's still mean," Kaycee retorted.

"To him, the clinic is business, not personal. He's not changing things out of spite."

"He doesn't know any of us, really," Kaycee said with a stubborn pout. "And he doesn't care. Anyway, there's nothing we can do about it. The rules say no one can win more than one handyman each year. You want Edgar and I have an apartment, so I don't need a handyman at all."

Darcy needed Edgar desperately. It might take all of what little she had in savings to win him—and even that might not be enough.

Potentially losing her job and trying to move away two months from now would be hard enough. Without his skills, it might be impossible to fix up the cottage enough to sell it in a few months.

But now empathy for Logan burned through her, taking a hard, painful hold of her heart. Could she stand by and let him become the humiliated laughingstock of the auction if no one bid even a few dollars?

She elbowed Kaycee sharply. "*Bid*," she whispered. "Now."

Startled, Kaycee stared at her. "What? I don't have the money."

"I'll pay. Bid against me just to bring it up to a decent amount so it isn't embarrassing for him, and then I'll take over. Seventy-five dollars max."

"Isn't this dishonest?"

"We'll be increasing the youth fund profits, not trying to get a deal," Darcy whispered back. "And I'll certainly honor my bid if I do win."

Kaycee weakly raised a hand to bid.

"We've got fifty, folks," the auctioneer cried out jubilantly. "Now, do we have seventy-five…"

Darcy nodded.

From across the room, she saw Gladys Rexworth eye her speculatively, and her heart sank.

"Eighty," the older woman barked. Her mouth twisted into a malevolent, superior smirk, and now Darcy realized this was personal.

Darcy closed her eyes briefly, remembering the run-ins she'd had with the woman in the past.

She hadn't wanted Logan to lose face in front of the community. But now this—this would be even worse. Gladys was a wealthy, spiteful woman who seemed to take pleasure in causing others grief with her wicked tongue.

Darcy didn't even want to imagine how Gladys might enjoy having the new vet under her thumb, and then spread her vicious comments after setting impossible standards for his work.

Darcy held Emma a little tighter and swallowed hard. "Eighty-five."

Gladys lifted her chin triumphantly. "Two hundred."

Please, God, tell me what to do here. Edgar stood next to the podium, awaiting his turn. The man who could swiftly, expertly deal with the most serious projects at the cottage…

Her shoulders sagged. "Two twenty-five."

Gladys's eyes widened and mouth narrowed. Then she shook her head.

"The vet is the bestseller so far tonight, folks," the auctioneer crowed. "And our lady vet is the winner! Could this mean there's a little romance in the air?"

Darcy groaned and ran a palm down her face at the titter of laughter in the audience.

"Now for the last opportunity of the night, we have…" The auctioneer droned on.

A sudden gasp spread through the crowd, and every head turned toward the back entrance.

Dr. Maxwell stood in the open doorway—windblown, disheveled and breathing hard, as if he'd run all the way from the clinic. His incredulous gaze shifted from the auctioneer to Darcy. "What on earth is going on here? I never—"

With Emma still in her arms, Darcy hurried to his side, looped an arm through his, and hauled him back outside. "Everything is fine, folks," she called over her shoulder. "He's just surprised to find he's worth that much. I sure am."

As she shut the door behind them, the auctioneer's delighted voice followed her outside. "Back to the highlight of the evening, folks. We have Edgar Larson, your last chance to bid. He's a fine carpenter who tops our auction every single year…"

She cringed inwardly. What in the world had she done?

Chapter Three

Her face pale, Darcy put her daughter down, leaned against the exterior wall of the church and closed her eyes. She looked as if she were on the verge of collapsing.

Her little girl gave Logan a wary look and hid behind her mom's legs, as if she thought he was the big bad wolf.

He moved a step closer in case Darcy crumpled to the ground. "Are you all right?"

"I can't believe I just did that," she moaned. She shot a sidelong glance at him. "I didn't plan to go that high, but then Gladys…"

"And I can't believe someone put my name on an auction block—and for what, I have no idea," Logan bit out. "I don't even know those people."

"*Those people* are members of this church, some of whom generously offered handyman skills, babysitting or hours of yard work to be sold at the annual handyman auction. The others are the generous folks in town who often pay far more than a deal is worth, because every dollar helps the youth group attend an annual faith rally in the Twin Cities," she retorted wearily. "If you'd answered my text messages on your cell, it wouldn't be at all confusing."

"I don't check my phone while driving."

"Not even at a gas station?" Now she sounded exasperated. "Or when you stop to eat?"

"I drove for several hours without good reception, and there *were* no messages."

"Then you need to switch cell companies."

The loud clang of metal against metal rang out from down the street. He glanced toward the sound. "That would be one of the horses in my trailer. I stopped at the clinic before going home and found a brief note on my desk that said, 'Auction at the church—be there at eight tonight,' so I came straight over here. Why am I involved in this?"

Her shoulders slumped. "My friend Beth is the committee chair, and she was desperate to have a few more names on the list. She also…um…thought it might give you some good PR in the community."

Beth, of course. He'd worked for days sorting and packing possessions to bring back to Wisconsin, hauling things to Goodwill and wrapping up the details of his old life in Montana.

Now, after fifteen hours in his truck, plus three long stops to unload the horses for a break from travel, all he wanted right now was to get them into the barn and collapse on his sofa. The coming week was going to be even more hectic…but now what had Beth gotten him into?

"So she just went ahead and added my name?"

"No. I told her I would ask you, but apparently her assistant added you at the last minute before running off the programs." Darcy shot a dark glance at him. "I suppose she figured that you—like all the others who volunteered—would be more than happy to help out the kids."

"And what does this involve, exactly?"

"The winning bidder gets twenty hours of your time—but it can be just a few hours here and there. Carpentry, home repairs, lawn care…whatever."

"So if I simply decline, you can save your money and I can save my time. Easy enough—"

A young woman with a long curly blond ponytail burst out of the building, headed straight for Darcy and pulled her into a brief hug. "I'm so sorry, honey. I was helping in the nursery, but heard about what happened in there—that you bid on someone no one else wanted. That was the kindest thing ever. I know how much you wanted Edgar instead."

No one else wanted? Logan didn't want to be in this situation at all, but hearing he didn't compare to some guy named Edgar didn't sit right, either. "Who's Edgar?"

Darcy ignored him. "Please—tell me Ed went for some impossible amount so I couldn't have won his bid anyway."

The woman bit her lower lip. "Two seventy-five."

Darcy's face fell. "Nooo."

"But remember, you'll never know how much higher the winner would have gone to beat you—it could have ended far, far above your budget."

Darcy scooped Emma up into her arms. "I'll keep that thought when I go back to trying to hire someone."

"Who knows? Maybe your guy has some great skills, too." The woman's speculative gaze swept over Logan.

"I don't think we've met. I'm Hannah Dorchester, one of the physician's assistants in town. And you are…"

"Logan Maxwell."

"So *you're* the one Darcy just bailed out, in front of all those people?"

Bewildered, he looked between the two of them. She'd bailed him out? "This was all a mistake. I'll go inside and straighten this out right away."

"Please don't make a scene." Hannah sidestepped to block the door. "The kids are all excited and celebrating. Anyway, it's all over now, so there's no rush. Go home. Think about it. Do you have any idea what Darcy just did for you?"

Darcy rested a hand on Hannah's forearm. "It's okay. He never agreed to this in the first place."

"I need to get back inside to help Beth wrap things up for the night." Hannah glanced at her watch, then tilted her head and gave Logan a brilliant smile. "Can I stop by the clinic for a few minutes first thing tomorrow? You can give me your decision then."

He gave a noncommittal nod, though he already knew what his answer would be.

Once she'd gone back into the building, he turned to Darcy, but at the sound of a horse delivering a another solid kick to the horse trailer, he reached for the keys he'd shoved in the back pocket of his jeans. "I'm being paged, so I'd better get those horses home."

She smiled at that. "Of course."

He would be free of this crazy situation tomorrow, no doubt about that. But all the way back to his new home, he couldn't escape the vision of Darcy's expression.

She'd been clearly embarrassed, but he'd also caught

a hint of desperation and bitter disappointment. So what was going on with her, for this auction to matter so much?

And who in the world was Edgar?

Hefting another bale of fragrant alfalfa that the farmer had just tossed down from the hay wagon, Logan looked over his shoulder at the approach of an unfamiliar car.

A moment later, the woman he'd met after the auction last night stepped out of the vehicle and approached him with a hand shading her eyes from the morning sun. Hannah, if he remembered correctly, though last night he'd been so tired he didn't know for sure.

"I called the clinic, but Marilyn said you were taking care of a hay delivery. So I decided I'd just bop out here. Beautiful drive, anyway, with all of this timber and those rocky bluffs. I always loved coming out to Doc's place for his annual barbecues."

"I could've saved you the trip if I'd had your number."

"That's why I wanted to see you in person." She laughed softly. "Beth and I are hoping you won't get off that easy."

"I'm sorry, but—"

"Honestly, I think you'd be better off if you just let it stand. Good PR and all that."

He tipped his head toward the house. "Even if I wanted to help y'all out, I just don't have the time. I can barely get in the door with all of the moving boxes stacked inside. It'll take days to finish fencing the pasture and longer to take care of repairs in the barn."

"But—"

"And then there's going to be extensive remodeling at the vet clinic. A lot of time just getting the new practice going, and we're still in foaling and breeding season, which means long days and even longer nights when I start seeing clients."

"Last year a guy backed out," Hannah said darkly, as if she hadn't heard a word about his complicated life. "It was the talk of the town for months when the winning bidder demanded her money back from the youth group, and that started a big flap about the future of the auction—liability, worries about lawsuits—but without this big fundraiser, too many deserving kids will miss a wonderful opportunity. This year we'd been praying there wouldn't be a single glitch to jeopardize the auction concept. But now there is. You."

"This reminds me of a conversation I had with Beth at the cafe." He stifled a laugh. "Darcy has some pretty convincing friends."

"My fiancé likes to say I'm forthright." Hannah rolled her eyes. "Others just say stubborn. But if it's for a good cause, why not?"

There were now a good twenty bales waiting for him on the ground. The man on top of the stack was holding another and eyeing him impatiently. "If that's it, then…"

He turned to get back to work, but she touched his arm. "Please."

"Look, I—"

"If you don't care about the kids, well…"

"It isn't that I don't care—I just don't have time."

"Then think about Darcy and what she gave up for you."

"What do you mean?"

"She's single, you know, with no family around to help. Her little cottage is a wreck, and she's been trying to hire a good handyman for months. But the good ones are booked 'til after the end of the year. And now, with her job in jeopardy since you showed up, she might have to sell and move. The cottage needs a *lot* of work before it can be listed."

Baffled, he shook his head slowly. "How could just twenty hours of labor make enough difference, then?"

"She wanted to win Edgar. She'd been saving for months, hoping he would get the work started and then be willing to keep working for her. He's a wonderful craftsman, but takes very few new clients."

"Then she shouldn't have bid on me."

"That's what I say. But she has a soft heart. She felt bad for you when no one else would bid. I'm sure she didn't want you to face any ridicule."

"I'm sure I could've handled it," he said dryly.

"Maybe so…but with half the town angry over you threatening to fire the entire vet clinic staff, why add more fuel to the fire? And—" Hannah bit her lower lip, as if deciding how much more to say "—the other woman who drove the bidding up is…well, I think Darcy went so high 'cause she was trying to save you from a potentially bad situation. Very bad."

The man on the hay wagon cleared his throat. "Hey, Doc, I need to get back to the farm. You want me to just keep pitching these off or what?"

Now there were a good fifty bales tossed into a jumbled pile on the ground, and at last one had landed wrong and broken. The farmer was muttering under his breath.

"I'll be with you in just a second."

He turned back to Hannah. "What if I made a donation to cover Darcy's bid instead of doing the work?"

Hannah folded her arms over her chest. "Fine, donate the two twenty-five. Except Darcy is still left high and dry. No Edgar, and no other skilled craftsmen are available until January…at least. Like I said, this is a small community."

"Fine. I'll do it, then," he said on a long sigh as he lifted a bale and started into the barn.

But long after Hannah left, questions kept spinning through his thoughts as he stacked bales into one of the box stalls he was using to store hay.

So Darcy had been struggling to save up for this auction? He knew what she was being paid at the clinic, and saving up a few hundred bucks for her beloved Edgar shouldn't have been any big deal.

Yet apparently she was strapped for cash.

So what was her problem? Credit card debt? A gambling problem? Sheer irresponsibility? She didn't seem like the type, but then, his own sister had mired herself in debt from online shopping, and he'd had to bail her out more than once so she and her kids wouldn't lose their condo.

And then there was his ex-fiancée—who had been far worse. He knew all too well how a person could be caught up in a web of embezzlement.

So maybe this unexpected situation wasn't so bad after all. If he completed the auction obligation to her, he'd have a chance to observe her situation and see if he even dared keep her around for the next two months.

Desperate people could end up doing desperate, illegal things, and he wasn't going through *that* situation ever again.

Logan logged onto the computer at the clinic on Monday morning and continued the search he'd started at home late last night.

"Marilyn, can you come in here, please?" he called out.

Darcy came in instead, wearing the new clinic uniform—maroon scrubs—plus her white lab coat with the Aspen Creek Vet Clinic logo on the front pocket, and a stethoscope around her neck. "She's out in the parking lot helping Mildred McConaughy bring her dog in. Can I help you?"

"I need to order some equipment, and I'd like an opinion on the vet supply distributor reps around here." He flipped through the battered Rolodex on the desk. "Who do you prefer to deal with?"

"Doc Boyd usually gave his orders to Harold Bailey— the two were old friends who went way back."

He looked up at her, momentarily taken aback. She stood in a shaft of morning sunlight streaming through the windows of his office. He'd first thought she had nondescript brown hair, but now he was struck by its rich, molten gold-and-amber highlights.

It took a moment to gather his scattered thoughts. "And…uh…you don't call him anymore?"

"His branch warehouse is clear down in the Quad Cities, and the company takes too long for deliveries. After Doc passed away, we started using ABC Vet Supply because it has a warehouse over in St. Paul. Next-day delivery, usually, because it's so close."

"So that sales rep is…" He thumbed back through the Rolodex. "Vicki Irwin?"

"She's young and fairly new, but sharp as can be and really follows through. She stops in twice a month. Sooner if we have any issues." Darcy lifted a shoulder in a faint shrug. "But of course, you'll need to decide for yourself which companies you want to use. What kind of equipment are you looking for?"

"The most outdated pieces of equipment are the blood chemistry machine and CBC cell counter—which should run around twenty grand. A new anesthesia machine would be at least four grand more."

"With Doc gone, I didn't feel right making any major purchases, but both are long overdue, for sure. What else?"

"Most everything else can wait a while." He shifted his gaze to the computer screen. "But a new equine ultrasound is imperative for reproductive issues and evaluating injuries."

She whistled under her breath. "Not cheap."

He nodded. "It could run over fifty grand if I duplicate what we used in Montana."

"It'll be fun watching you bring this clinic up to date." She turned to leave, but he cleared his throat. "Your friend Hannah came out to see me on Saturday. I imagine she told you about it."

"What?" Her mystified expression cleared. "You mean about the auction? I knew she planned to talk to you, but I haven't heard from her since Friday night."

"She and I got everything squared away."

"Good to hear. I told Beth that the committee shouldn't try to push you into something you never intended to do, so you're off the hook."

"But is that what you want? Your friend says you've been saving money for this for a long time." He eyed her closely. "That you really need the help and can't find anyone to do it."

"Yes, well…that's my concern, not yours." A weary smile briefly lit up her face, and she looked like someone who had the weight of the world on her shoulders. "Honestly, I just want to apologize for what happened."

"I understand your bidding saved me from the clutches of a difficult woman."

At that, she laughed aloud. "You do owe me a favor for that. You have no idea."

"I'm going to follow through. Will that just about cover it?"

Her eyes widened with surprise and a touch of wariness. "You don't need to. Really."

"I called Beth just a few minutes ago. It's a done deal."

"Um…" Her gaze veered away, and she swallowed hard. "I don't mean to seem ungrateful, but I…um… need someone who is really skilled as a handyman. Experienced."

"You're worried about getting your money's worth." He heard the unintentionally hard edge in his tone and instantly regretted it when he saw her flinch.

"I must sound so crass." Rosy color washed up into her cheeks. "It's just that whether my daughter and I stay or need to leave town, I… I need the work to be done well and up to code."

"Tell you what. You've got twenty hours of my time, so make a list of what needs to be done. Then let me come over some evening this week so I can see if I have the skill set for what you need. Tonight would be fine, if you're eager to get started."

"That I am." She bit her lower lip. "But if you don't feel it's something you want to tackle?"

"Then I'll donate the full amount of your bid to the youth group, and you can save your money to pay someone else." He offered his hand across the desk. "Deal?"

She hesitated, her expression still filled with doubt,

but she finally accepted his brief handshake. "This is beyond generous. I think you're being too kind."

Not kind, he thought as he watched her head out of his office. *Just careful.*

Since asking about her around town would only start rumors, he needed to take this into his own hands.

Because absolute trust was a rare and fragile thing, and he couldn't afford to make the same mistake twice.

Chapter Four

Darcy had given Logan a list of projects and the directions to her house before leaving work at the end of the day. She'd blushed a little, saying she knew there were far more than twenty hours of labor on the list, but she'd thought he might want to choose what he wanted to do.

A tactful expectation that he'd need to select the easier tasks, he supposed.

From that long, long list he'd figured she was living in shabby house worthy of a wrecking ball in a seedy part of town. Probably around the taverns, trailer park and mechanic's shop on the south end.

But he'd followed her directions down several winding, tree-shaded streets into an area of well-kept homes from the early 1900s. Now he stood on the sidewalk in front of 56 Cranberry Lane and just stared.

The surrounding houses were two-story brick, with sweeping covered porches on the front, leaded glass and manicured lawns. Darcy's place was brick as well, but just a single story, with a brick-paved driveway leading past the side of the house to a matching one-stall garage.

It reminded him of a dollhouse in comparison. A neglected one, at that. If Darcy was blowing her money, it hadn't been spent on the place she lived.

Lace curtains in the front window fluttered. Then the door opened and Darcy came across the porch and down the steps and let him through the gate at edge of the sidewalk.

"I'm sure you can already see some of the projects here," she said with a self-conscious laugh, gesturing at the ornate white picket fence surrounding the front yard. "The backyard is fenced as well, and there must be dozens of pickets that have broken or rotted away."

He eyed the intricately cut upright pieces. "These were custom-made."

"My sweet old aunt loved detail. There are lots and lots of gingerbread trim pieces on the cottage, and she echoed that theme in the fence." Darcy smiled fondly. "I loved visiting her, because the place was rather like a little fairyland theme park. Lots of animal and elf statues tucked away in unexpected places, some little goldfish ponds. But now I can't just go to a lumberyard and pick up replacements. She wanted everything to be unique."

He glanced up at the house. "Your aunt…"

"She passed away almost two years ago and left everything to my brother and me. He essentially got her liquid assets, and I got the cottage. So when I was able to find a job in town, I was thrilled."

"Did you grow up here?"

"North of Minneapolis, actually. But after…" Her voice trailed off. "Well. Let's take a quick look around, okay? I put Emma to bed a few minutes ago, and I need to get back inside."

She took him around the house, pointing out broken gingerbread trim along the eaves and a sagging rear porch, then took him through the back door into the kitchen.

The cupboards and countertops were dated and worn, with a circular burn mark on the counter next to the stove. The vinyl flooring was yellowed and scarred with age. The room was small.

But a row of four sash windows looked out on the backyard, giving it an airy, quaint feel, and the burnished oak woodwork glowed in the light of a stained-glass chandelier that hung over the oak claw-foot table.

"As you can see, there is no end to the projects around here. I can't afford to remodel the kitchen fully, but the sink and faucet need replacing, and the lighting in here is impossible. It's like working in a cave." She led him through an archway leading into a small living room and gestured to the left. "That door leads to two bedrooms and a bathroom. The first priority inside is the carpet, because of Emma's asthma. Fortunately there's beautiful old oak flooring throughout the house, but it needs to be refinished, and there's quite a bit of work in the bathroom, too."

"Your other priorities?"

"Everything," she said simply. "I'd love to remodel the entire place if I could, but anything you want to tackle and have time to finish would be wonderful. I don't expect even a minute extra. I'm just grateful, given all that you have on your own plate."

He turned slowly, taking in the faded floral wallpaper, the lacy curtains and the worn leather furniture that made him think of soft marshmallows. A small television sat in one corner with a DVD player and stack of children's DVDs on top. No high-end electronics here.

"So if you'd won the bid on your friend, you might have gotten everything done?"

"Edgar isn't a friend, but I did hope to convince him to stay on longer for his usual rate. Whether he would've agreed or not, I've no idea."

"Well, I'll do everything I can. You can decide where to start."

"Really—you can do this?"

At the renewed doubt in her voice, he stifled a chuckle. "I'm sure I can't compare to Edgar, but I grew up on an isolated ranch where we dealt with most everything on our own. And then I put myself through college working summers for a contractor."

"Really?" The worried look in her eyes faded. "Perfect. I'd like to start with the picket fence, because it would really improve the curb appeal. Maybe that isn't possible, though. Those swirly edges and the heart cutouts at the top of the pickets must be tricky."

"No problem. I've got a band saw and a jigsaw, and I can use an old picket as a template."

"I realize the fence might take a good part of your hours, but with whatever time is left, can you start work on the kitchen?"

"No problem."

From one of the bedrooms came the faint sound of Emma whimpering.

"Sounds like you're needed, and I'd better get home to do my horse chores." Logan pulled his truck keys from his back jeans pocket as he headed for the door. "Just figure out where you want to start, and I'll come back after work tomorrow to do some measuring. I'll write up a list of materials, and once you have them, I can get to work."

The enormity of the work to be done here and her concern about it were more than clear. He felt a twinge of guilt as he walked out to his pickup.

He'd been in seminars at vet conferences where business consultants recommended making a clean sweep of things, bringing in new staff unencumbered with prior loyalties and stubborn adherence to old routines.

So when he made an offer on the clinic, he hadn't thought too deeply about what his plans would mean to the current staff. His focus had been on new beginnings—financing and building a successful new practice.

If he'd been empathetic enough to consider the collateral effect on the people involved, would he have turned down this chance to start his life over?

And would he now change his plans for the focused vet practice he'd always wanted—what he had specialized in through an extended equine medicine residency and then pursued in the Montana group practice for the past eight years?

That was another question.

"Thanks, Logan—have a good night," Darcy called softly from the door as she closed it.

He stared at the door after she turned off the front light, sorting out his thoughts. She was certainly an enigma.

She was a single mom, which had to be tough. Yet she did have a good career, she'd inherited this house and he'd seen no evidence of profligate spending. If she was as strapped for cash as Hannah had implied on Saturday, where was her money going? Was she a risk as an employee?

He hadn't known her for very long, but while his

heart told him no, the logical, analytical side of his brain said yes.

She was the spitting image of the associate vet who had so easily ruined his life in Montana, the one who had so quickly captured his heart. Was that why he felt an inexplicable tug of emotion whenever he ran into her? A physical awareness tinged with a persistent niggle of doubt?

Whatever he felt about her, it had no place in his life. Not now, not ever.

The humiliating interrogations, legal fees and defamation of his character back in Montana were too fresh in his mind to take any chances.

Darcy finished her exam of the Chihuahua and smiled. "Scooter is doing really well. The X-rays show excellent healing."

Mrs. Johnson picked her dog up and cuddled him against her chest. "I was so worried—I don't know what I'd do without my little boy for company."

"You made the right choice when you let me go ahead with the plating and bone graft. Splinting of radius-ulna fractures in these small dogs doesn't always succeed."

"Worth every penny to do things right, I always say." She gave the little dog a kiss on its head.

Darcy handed her a list of going-home instructions. "You said that he always wants to be on the sofa and bed with you. Have you set up some ramps for him? He shouldn't be jumping to the floor."

"I ordered two from a catalog, and they were delivered yesterday." The elderly woman moved toward the door, then turned back with a wink and a smile. "I heard about you winning the new vet at the handyman auction, and I just think it's so sweet. Smart, too, keeping all of the other young ladies at bay like that. Keep him to yourself."

Darcy swallowed hard. "Believe me, that really isn't it at all—"

"Your secret is safe with me." Mrs. Johnson waggled her eyebrows and gave her a knowing look. "Can we assume romance is already in the air?"

"No." Darcy briefly closed her eyes against *that* unwanted vision. "Not at all. Really."

But judging by her smug little smile and the teasing sparkle in her eyes as she left the exam room, Mrs. Johnson didn't believe a word of that denial and wasn't planning to keep her thoughts to herself, either.

Darcy braced her hands on the exam table. Word would spread. People would believe she'd made a pathetic effort to snare the new vet. Maybe Logan would believe it, too, which would be beyond embarrassing.

Marilyn rapped lightly on the door frame. "I've got your next two charts, and—oh, my. Is everything all right? You look a bit pale."

"I'm fine." Darcy straightened. "Just reminding myself that small-town gossip doesn't mean a thing."

Marilyn flicked a hand dismissively. "You mean about you and Dr. Maxwell?"

Darcy groaned. "You do know it's completely false conjecture, no matter where you've heard it?"

"I guessed that already, given that he's probably planning to let us all go during the next few months," Marilyn retorted dryly. "But when you won that bid at the auction, there were lots of whispers going through the crowd. That was bound to happen anyway, with both of you being single and all. People like to talk."

Darcy glanced at the clock on the wall. "Wednesday afternoons usually aren't this busy, but I've been swamped all day. Has he come in?"

"He's been out back working on that old stable and corral all day, far as I know." She handed Darcy the charts. "Kaycee has your next client in the other exam room, but if you need to talk to him, I can go out and let him know."

"No, I'll catch him later. He came over after work yesterday to take measurements for my fence, and I just wanted to let him know that I bought the materials at the lumberyard."

Marilyn's eyebrows rose with sudden hope. "Sooo… are you two getting along a little better?"

Darcy snorted.

"Seriously," Marilyn said. "Maybe if we're all really professional and helpful, he'll decide that we're worth keeping around. *All* of us," she added pointedly.

"I don't think being friendly will change his business plans, but go for it and see what happens. As far as I know, he still doesn't plan to make his final decisions until around June 14—at the end of two months."

"When I think of all the accessibility issues Bob had at our house, and all we've done to make it better for him…" Marilyn bit her lower lip and looked away. "I'm just praying I can keep this job and our house, because Bob's Parkinson's is not going away."

Over the past year, Marilyn had been the motherly one at the office, giving Darcy comfort and advice during her darkest days. Now the tables had turned and Darcy was the one comforting the older woman.

Darcy set aside the charts and gave the older woman a quick hug. "I can't believe there could be any issue with keeping you and Kaycee on board, honestly. If anyone will be packing her bags, it will be me."

"Oh, honey. That would be so wrong."

Darcy stepped back and sighed. "If that happens, then I figure the Lord has better plans for me. I've been thinking harder about starting my own practice here in town. But right now, I'd better get back to work."

At the sound of a nearby footstep, Marilyn turned and paled. "D-Dr. Maxwell," she stammered. "I didn't see you coming."

"Just taking a quick break." If he'd overheard their conversation, there was no sign of it in his voice. "Have you had any calls or emails about the new website?

Flustered, Marilyn fiddled with her bracelet. "Three calls, just this afternoon. I left the messages on your desk. There have been some emails, as well."

Darcy stepped into the hallway to head for the other exam room, but faltered to a stop.

The days and nights were still cool in Wisconsin, and she'd seen him wear just jeans and sweaters or sweatshirts so far. But now he was in a ragged T-shirt and well-worn jeans, dusted with sawdust.

The T-shirt stretched across his powerful chest. The short sleeves clung to his powerful biceps. His tool belt was once again slung low around his hips.

The man could work as a model if he ever wanted an easier profession.

She forced her gaze up to his face. "Sounds like good news for you, then. The potential clients, I mean."

"I updated the new website to show the equine practice will be open starting on Monday, but in the meantime I'd be happy to take calls from anyone curious about available services. Feel free to give them my cell number."

Marilyn nodded and fled back to the receptionist's desk, leaving Darcy facing Logan alone.

"She sure is jumpy," he said mildly.

"She's terribly worried about her job, and Kaycee is, as well," Darcy said in a low voice. "They both have heavy responsibilities at home. It would be a kindness if you could let them know your plans and get the news over with."

He assessed her with a frank, open gaze. "And what about you?"

She shrugged, locked her gaze on his. "I'll either be working here or move down the road and become your toughest competition. The choice is yours."

Chapter Five

"Is he coming today?" Emma ran to the front door for the fourth time in the past ten minutes, her blond ponytail flying. "With his horse? The one that's blonde like me? Maybe it could stay overnight, or even live with us!"

Darcy had left the vet clinic when it closed at noon, picked up Emma at the sitter and had been trying to settle the little girl down for lunch, to no avail. "No horses, not in town. Not even briefly, because horses need a very good fence, and ours needs lots of work. That's why Dr. Maxwell is coming."

Emma's face fell. "Could we go see it, then? And ride it?"

"Um...maybe someday. Two more bites of your sandwich. Then we'll go outside and get things ready for him. All right?"

Emma dutifully clambered up onto her chair and took two miniscule bites, then raced for the back door. "Then can we get a puppy? You promised, after Elsie died."

Keeping up with Emma sometimes made Darcy's

head spin. "Yes, I did. But not until our fence is completely done. We always had to take Elsie for walks, but a nice safe yard would be much better than taking those walks after dark."

"Can you ask Hannah? She has lots and lots of puppies. Cats, too. And a *pony*." Emma's face brightened with excitement. "A pony could stay in our yard!"

Emma asked about horses and ponies every day, from morning 'til night. "When you turn five, we'll look for a pony and a place to keep it. Right now, let's think about a puppy. One thing at a time."

She grabbed a hammer from the utility closet by the back door and followed the little girl out into the yard. She breathed in deeply, savoring the scents of the neighbor's fresh-cut grass and the spring perennials Aunt Tina had planted along the borders of the yard years ago.

Yellow crocuses, grape hyacinths and daffodils nodded cheerfully in the light breeze. Soon the sweet scent of lilacs—her favorite—would fill the air, followed later by the heady scents of the heirloom roses planted on three sides of the tiny brick gardening shed.

All of them brought back bittersweet memories of her aunt and those carefree days of childhood when everything seemed possible and nothing bad had ever happened. Yet.

"Can I help you, Mommy?"

"Why don't you play on your swing set for a while? I'm going to start taking down the broken pickets, and nails are very sharp."

She'd just pried off the first splintered picket when Emma shrieked. "He came—he really came!"

Her heart in her throat, Darcy spun around…and saw Logan saunter through the backyard gate with a stack of boards in his arms and his tool belt slung around his hips once again.

Every time she saw him, she felt a little frisson of awareness, and her traitorous heart seemed to skip a beat. It had to be the jeans and cowboy boots, and that casual cowboy grace suggesting he could drawl *yes, ma'am* and then vanquish her foes with no effort at all.

If only he'd met her late husband, Dean, she would have loved to see him try.

Emma raced to the gate. "Are you a real cowboy?" she asked, looking up at him with adoration she rarely showed to anyone except Darcy anymore. "Did you bring your horse? Mommy says no, but maybe you did anyway."

He chuckled and grinned down at her, the corners of his eyes crinkling and that dimple deepening in his cheek. "Your mom is right, but someday you can come out to my place and we'll see about letting you ride. Would that be okay?"

Darcy strolled over. If only the man knew what he had just started with that little offer.

"Thanks for coming," she called out. "I'm sure you had other ways you wanted to spend your Saturday afternoon."

"No problem." He stacked the pickets on the wrought iron table under a shady oak. "I have more in my truck, but what do you think so far?"

She ran her hand over the smooth, one-by-four pressure-treated slats that the lumberyard guy had promised would hold up for years. Each swoop and curlicue along the edges was exactly right; the little heart cutouts near the top of each pointed tip were a perfect match to the originals.

"They're beautiful," she said with awe. "How in the world did you do them so fast?"

He shrugged. "Having the right equipment helped."

Emma looked up at him, her eyes hopeful. "Could you make a playhouse, like Sienna has?" she breathed. "Her daddy made it. It's pink and white and has a purple roof. But I don't got a daddy."

"Dr. Maxwell only has enough time to help with the fencing and fix some things in the house, Emma. We need the fence before we can think about your puppy. Remember?"

"But—"

"Let's help him fetch the rest of his things. He and I need to get to work. Okay?"

Emma dutifully followed them out to the black pickup parked in front of the garage, where Logan gave her a single picket to carry. Then Darcy and Logan took the remaining pickets and his tools to the backyard.

Emma watched for a while, then wandered back to her outdoor slide and swing set and played on the upper deck with her dolls.

With Darcy removing damaged pickets and Logan using an electric drill to set the new ones, they were finished with the front yard and backyard a couple of hours later.

"I could've painted them before bringing them over," he said, stepping back to assess the overall job. "But I figured it would be better to do the entire fence all at once, after the peeling paint is scraped. Do you want me to do that or start something else?"

"This is just beautiful," she said fervently. She bit her lower lip, thinking about all of the work he'd done back at his shop. "I can do the painting later on. I'm not even sure how much of your time I have left, though, given what you've done already."

"Eighteen hours would be fair enough." He shrugged. "Does that work for you?"

"But you spent more than two hours just putting it up today. And what about all of the time you spent making the pickets? That isn't fair to you."

"It was simple, and I like woodworking. It was a nice break from working on the barn at home and the one at the clinic. Gave me an excuse to avoid unpacking boxes in the house, too," he added with a grin. "Just forget about it."

He'd been gruff and cold when he'd arrived two weeks ago. She'd been prepared to dislike him completely after that first awkward encounter. But she'd started to see a different side of him now, and it was getting harder to keep up her defenses. Especially when he was so sweet to Emma and being such a good sport about this whole arrangement.

"Thank you," she said quietly. "This means a lot to me."

He glanced at his watch. "Let's go inside and figure out the next project before I head back home."

He and Emma followed her into the kitchen, where he leaned a hip against the counter and surveyed the room. "Not sure how far you want to go with this. The material costs will add up. Do you have a budget in mind?"

"Not really. I can't afford a lot right now, though."

"Are you planning to take out any walls?"

"No. I want a separation between the living room and kitchen. And the layout is fine."

"Do you want to replace the cabinets?"

She laughed at that. "I've spent a lot of time pricing cabinets. No way."

"You could just install updated cabinet fronts at a fraction of the cost." He ran a hand over a cabinet door and opened several of them. "You could add new veneer over the exposed sides and then add new doors. Or you paint or stain the ones you have. These are outdated, but they're well made. You could add nicer hardware, too. Once you decide that, you could consider new countertops."

"They definitely need updating. These are nicked and faded—and that big burn mark by the stove drives me crazy."

"Granite would be nice."

"In my dreams," she said ruefully.

"Sometimes you can find nice pieces of granite that were ordered for a larger kitchen and didn't work out but would fit in a small space, and that could save you a lot of money. You could call some suppliers to see if there's anything you like. Then we'd measure carefully, and it would be cut and delivered. I could install a new sink and faucet."

Excitement over the possibilities started bubbling up in her chest. "Or should I do the lighting instead?

He studied the ceiling. "You have an attic up there, so there should be good access into the ceiling for can lighting. If this were my place, I'd go ahead and do it myself, but I'm not a licensed electrician. That's who you need to call. A wild guess is that it would cost between five hundred and a thousand, depending on how many lights you want and where you buy them. Then again, I have no idea what the going rates are around here."

"What about the floor?" she asked.

"Are you sure there's hardwood underneath the vinyl?"

"I've pulled up some corners of the carpeting in all of the other rooms and also pried up a corner of the vinyl," she said. "It's all narrow-plank oak."

"It wouldn't be hard to rip out the carpet and vinyl and refinish the floors. That needs to be a priority, given Emma's asthma. But if you help, we could get that done and maybe do the counters and sink, as well."

Incredulous, she looked up at him. "Really? Wow. So many options."

She closed her eyes for a moment, envisioning what these changes would mean. How pretty the cottage could become, inside and out. She took another look around, and the possibilities nearly took her breath away.

A smile twitched at his lips as he watched her consider. "No rush if you want to think it over. But if you can decide fairly soon, we can tackle the work before I start getting busy with clients."

"Okay—the floor. Definitely the floor." She grinned up at him. "I think you've just made me the happiest woman in Aspen Creek, bar none. When do you want to start?"

"Tomorrow is okay, or some night after work."

"We have church, and Sunday school for Emma tomorrow morning." She gave him a tentative smile. "Aspen Creek Community Church, if you're interested. The service is at nine."

"No." He drew back a little. "Maybe another time."

"Of course," she murmured. "We'll be home all afternoon and evening if you want to stop by. Lunch is around noon if you want to join us."

* * *

Logan spent Sunday morning finishing up his work on the small horse barn behind the vet clinic and regretting his surly response to Darcy's invitation.

He'd been raised in the church. His parents had made sure of that.

And he was a believer, even if he and God had gone through a major falling-out a few years back when Dad passed away from a heart attack and Mom died shortly after. Two of the best people he'd ever known, gone in the blink of an eye. Logan had prayed night and day that they might survive, but God hadn't seen fit to answer those prayers.

Where was the justice in that, when truly evil people could spend their entire lives loose in society?

His prayers sure hadn't helped with the situation in Montana, either. Since God didn't seem to find his prayers worth answering, Logan had simply...stopped praying.

He stepped back and studied his handiwork. The barn had originally been divided into four fourteen-by-fourteen box stalls, with an exam area with stocks to restrain horses during certain procedures, and a space for hay, bedding and feed storage. He'd repaired and replaced boards, painted the interior white, and installed long banks of fluorescent lights over the stalls and exam area. In time he would add a surgical room with a hydraulic table and more stalls, but this would be a good start.

He glanced at his watch. Grabbed his truck keys and headed out the door. His work commitment at Darcy's place was just that—a business agreement and nothing more. Once he finished those eighteen hours, he would be back to concentrating on his career and the work he was doing on his place in the country. Back to enjoying his life alone.

So why did he find himself whistling as he drove off toward Cranberry Lane? Or fidgeting with his keys like some nervous teenage boy after he knocked on her door?

It made absolutely no sense at all.

Chapter Six

The last time he'd seen her, Darcy had proclaimed she was the happiest woman in Aspen Creek. On Sunday afternoon she looked a little worse for wear.

Her long hair was caught up into a straggly knot on the top of her head, with long tendrils dangling down her back. Her ragged T-shirt and torn jeans were covered with dust. There was a smudge on her nose. A mask hung from its elastic cord around her neck.

He'd never seen her look so...so vulnerable and pretty and, well, so utterly appealing. But then he looked a little closer. A number of wounds on her hands were haphazardly covered with adhesive bandages.

"What on earth happened to you?"

"I followed your advice. Sort of." She waved a hand toward the living room behind her.

He took a closer look at her hands. "Whatever advice it was, I had to be wrong."

She stepped aside to let him in, and he nearly tripped over a heap of musty carpeting and shreds of carpet pad.

"I figured you could get more of the technical stuff done if I did all of the demolition. So I looked up the process on YouTube, and I've been pulling up carpet. I figured that the sooner I got rid of that dusty, musty stuff, the better it would be for Emma." She abruptly turned away to sneeze. "I had some run-ins with tack strips around the borders, though. The video didn't give any warning about that. And it didn't say that some people might take it upon themselves to fasten the padding down with an ocean of glue. That was an unpleasant surprise."

He glimpsed a pile of furniture in the kitchen. "I could have done this. You should have let me."

Speechless now, he moved farther into the room. She'd managed to pull up all of the carpet and most of the padding, but random patches of padding were still stuck to the floor, and she held a scraper in her hand as if ready to go back to war.

"Someone—not my aunt—did a sloppy job of painting the walls before laying the carpet. There are big splotches all over the hardwood." She gave him an impish smile, her eyes twinkling. "But I also learned about drum sanders and edging sanders on the video, and I got both rented last night just before the lumberyard closed."

His jaw dropped. "When did you do all of this?"

"I took Emma to Hannah's for an overnight because there was so much dust and mold in the air. Then I worked until around three this morning and after I got home from church."

"I'm impressed."

"I've got to finish all of the bits of padding stuck to the floor, but I shifted furniture around so I could at least get all of the carpeting out." She blew at a strand of hair drooping over one eye. "So, what do you think?"

He angled an amused smile at her. "If anyone ever doubted your work ethic, that thought would be laid to rest. Where do you want me to start?"

"I can keep pulling carpet tacks and scraping the floors in here, but if you want to start on the vinyl flooring in the kitchen, that would be super. This house is so small that I think I can get all of the floors sanded and return the sanders tomorrow morning if I just keep at it."

"No problem."

"Are you sure you don't mind? I feel kinda bad asking you to take on a job like that. I'm guessing the floor is nasty under the vinyl. Then again, maybe this will be a good coworker bonding experience. Right?"

There'd been an invisible wall between them since he first arrived—mutual wariness, at the very least. How could there not be, when he'd initially planned to let her go, and she'd finagled another two months at her job? But working on her house together was slowly easing those tensions, and this was becoming almost…fun.

He grabbed an armload of carpet and carried it out to the pile she'd started by the garage, then kept taking loads of it outside until it was gone.

He started for the kitchen, then headed for the back hallway and bedrooms where Darcy was still pulling stray carpet tacks along the baseboards and prying off ancient bits of rubber carpet pad.

In here, evidence of garish yellow and pink paint splotches trailed across the floor. "Must have been sort of psychedelic," he observed. "But the woodwork is beautiful."

"My aunt moved here in 1978 and had it all redone in vintage wallpaper, as you can see. She loved flowers and calico. And lace. Lots and lots of lace." Darcy sat back on her heels. "So I'll be doing a lot of wallpaper stripping, which I hear is as much fun as this carpet."

He turned to head for the kitchen but spied a white cord dangling just a few inches above his head and looked up. "There must be access to the attic through that trap door. Have you ever been up there?"

She shook her head. "Just once as a kid. I remember there were lots of trunks and boxes crammed in every corner. But I assumed there were lots of spiders and bats, so I didn't linger."

"Want me to check to see how easy it would be to install the can lights for the kitchen?"

Still crouched along the baseboards, she looked over her shoulder. "Be my guest. The bathroom is just to your left, and I've got a flashlight charging in the outlet near the sink. Be careful, though—I don't know how long it's been since anyone went up there. I hope the ladder is still safe."

He grabbed the flashlight, jammed it into his back pocket and studied the dangling cord. "This has got to be one of those folding staircases. Right?"

"Yep."

He reached up and gently tugged the cord. Nothing moved. Reaching up with his other hand in case the ladder apparatus came down too quickly, he gave the cord another tug. Nothing.

"It's jammed. I need to get a stepladder and check this out—"

A deceptively lazy swirl of dust drifted downward like the flakes in a snow globe.

Metal squealed.

The screech of twisting, splintering wood filled the air.

Logan pivoted to get out of the way, but the mass of metal framework and heavy oak above him lurched downward, then crashed to the floor, knocking him flat.

Stars exploded behind his eyelids, and then the room went black.

"This really wasn't necessary," Logan grumbled as Dr. McClaren left the room. "I told you he would let me go home."

In his jeans and a hospital gown that barely stretched across his chest, he seemed to overwhelm the cramped ER cubicle. Darcy had been prepared to stop him if he tried to leave before the doctor showed up. She'd already tucked his boots under her chair and out of sight.

"But you were knocked out."

"For just a minute. No big deal."

"Except that you do have a mild concussion, and that *is* a big deal. And then there's that arm."

"It's fine." He started to stretch but suddenly winced and grabbed for his injured right shoulder.

"I can see it's perfectly fine," she retorted dryly. "No pain at all."

He glowered at her. "It'll be good by tomorrow. It has to be."

After a physical exam, an X-ray and a range-of-motion evaluation, Dr. McClaren had said there were no fractures, but he suspected a partially torn rotator cuff. He'd recommended a sling and minimal use of the arm, and if the shoulder pain wasn't alleviated by NSAIDs or a prescription pain med, an MRI and surgical repair might be next on the list.

"You know the doc is right about taking it easy for

a while. And if you think you'll be seeing equine patients tomorrow, that's a no."

When he eased off the gurney, she helped him shove his feet into his boots. He turned away and awkwardly attempted to put on his T-shirt, but the complexity of doing it with one good arm and a painful shoulder on the other side clearly confounded him. For just a moment, he seemed to sway on his feet.

"Here, let me." Darcy briskly stepped forward and helped him get it on, trying to ignore the intimacy of this moment as she smoothed it down over his broad shoulders. "Are you going to be all right at home?"

He snorted. "Of course."

"Too bad it's your right shoulder. Do you have anyone to stay with you tonight? And what about your horse chores?"

"No problem," he said wearily, rubbing a hand down his face. "I can manage."

"Right. Can you even drive?"

"He'd better not." One of the nurses bustled in, a clipboard in hand. "And yes, he should have someone with him tonight because he had a pretty good rap on the head."

She demonstrated the use of a sling, but he waved it away. Then she ran through his going-home instructions and handed over the printed copy along with a script for a prescription pain med. "No refills on this one. It has to be filled with a physical prescription in hand. I can't call it in to the pharmacy. Do you need a wheelchair to the ER entrance?"

Logan gave her an appalled look. "No, ma'am."

"I can drive you home," Darcy offered when the nurse gave him a last disgruntled look and left the room.

"We can run out to do your chores and pick up Emma on the way back to my house." Darcy frowned, thinking about the disaster that was now her home, with furniture still piled in corners. "It'll take me just a few minutes to set up the bedrooms again. Emma can sleep in my room, and you can have hers for the night."

He shook his head. "That's too much trouble. In fact, I could take a taxi home and save you the trip."

"There are no taxis here. And the doctor said—"

"Patients do have rights, and it's my decision. I'm going home."

"You know, my friend Keeley's fiancé had a similar head injury once, and I remember him being a lot more agreeable." Darcy rolled her eyes. "But it's your brain, so go ahead and ignore my offer and my greater wisdom. Good luck."

Out at Logan's place in the country an hour later, Darcy brought his two horses into the barn, grained them and waited in the cool, dark aisle while they ate.

Logan leaned a hip against a stall door and breathed in the clean, familiar scents of alfalfa, leather and horse, his gaze on Darcy. "Thanks for helping me out."

"There was no question at all. I owe you this and more." She turned to look at him. "I'm so sorry that you got hurt. You were only being kind by helping me, and the accident was my fault. I expect you to file a claim with my homeowner's insurance for bills, by the way. I'll call them first thing tomorrow morning."

"You couldn't have known about that ladder apparatus. If it had fallen on you, you might have been killed."

"Because you have a harder head?" she teased.

"I'm a lot taller, and I was already reaching upward. I was able to deflect some of the impact."

"I'm just praying that you heal quickly so your shoulder doesn't hold you back for very long. I...called Marilyn, by the way."

He felt himself tense. "And?"

"You have some appointments tomorrow morning. Two families with 4-H kids needing health papers for their horses, so they can attend a horse project workshop next weekend. Both horses already have current, negative Coggins test results and vaccination records, So now they just need the exams."

"I can handle that."

"As can I, if your shoulder is even more painful tomorrow. It probably will be. And you have a presale soundness exam in the afternoon."

He smiled wryly. "Not exactly land office business."

"For your first day? It's a good start. I'm impressed. I understand there's been a strong response on the website, too. What else are you doing?"

"Two of the local saddle clubs have asked me to speak at their monthly meetings, and I'll be writing an article for the state quarter horse association newsletter next month. I also started a Twitter account as Aspen Creek Equine Clinic, so I figure word will start spreading."

Even in the shady gloom of the barn, he saw her stiffen. "Have you already changed the name?"

"Not yet. I think I found the right vet box to put on my truck for farm calls. Guess I'll need to decide on the name so it can be painted on the side."

She fell silent, and the temperature in the barn seemed to drop thirty degrees.

"I see," she said finally as she looked into the two stalls where the horses had finishing eating and were now heads-down, snuffling around in the cedar shaving bedding. She snapped a lead rope on the palomino's halter and led her back to the pasture, then took the gelding outside. "I've got to pick up Emma and head for home. Do you need anything else?"

"No, but thanks." He straightened and followed her out to her car. "I'll get back to finishing up my hours at your place soon as I can."

"After discovering the wonders of YouTube educational videos, I now realize I can do the floors just fine by myself, which will keep my nights busy for a while." She waved a hand dismissively. "And I'll call around to ask some electricians for estimates on the lighting. Everything else can wait. Don't worry about it—I've got a lot of other things to think about in the meantime."

Chapter Seven

As Darcy predicted and he'd known full well himself—
not that he'd wanted to admit it to her—Logan's painful shoulder kept him awake all night and felt worse the
next day.

She picked him up the next morning since his truck
was still at her place. After the drive to the clinic, his
shoulder was even more uncomfortable. He grudgingly
asked her to cover the 4-H horse exams after realizing with chagrin that the first one, a black Welsh pony
owned by the Fowlers, was noticeably lame, and some
of the steps of a lameness evaluation would be nearly
impossible with his own injured shoulder.

He quietly watched from the sidelines in the fenced
courtyard behind the clinic as Darcy went through each
of the flexion tests meant to isolate sources of pain in
the joints and soft tissue.

One by one, she lifted each back hoof and held the
leg in a cramped, flexed position for sixty seconds, then
watched as Kaycee led the gelding away at a trot. Then
Darcy used a hoof tester on each foot.

After she completed the rest of the exam, she smiled

at the young girl and her father. "You have a lovely pony, Anna."

"Is Pepper okay?" The girl cast a worried look at the pony. "Can I take him to the workshop?"

"Right now he's too lame. I saw him last summer, and he was sore even then. We took X-rays of his feet, remember? We figured out that he easily grass-founders, so I talked about what you needed to do. Have you kept him off the pasture?"

Anna nodded vigorously. "I bring him in the barn every night."

"But—"

"That's right," her father interjected. "He's out there only nine or ten hours at the most."

A pained expression flickered in Darcy's eyes. "Was he sound over the fall and winter?"

Anna nodded again.

"That's because your pasture was winter brown. He didn't have rich green grass then—which is especially troublesome for a horse with this problem. His tendency for founder will always be the worst in the spring. Right now, both of his front feet are very warm and painful, and I can feel a strong pulse. I'm going to give him an injection to alleviate that pain for now and give you a tube of the pain medicine you used last year. And no more green grass for this boy. Promise?"

Kaycee ran into the clinic and returned with the syringe.

Anna looked away while Darcy administered the medication, and she dug her toe in the dirt. "Dad says he has to be in the pasture to eat, 'cause we don't need to buy hay for him in the summer. It's a waste of money."

Mr. Fowler cleared his throat, his face reddening.

"Why let all that pasture go to waste, right? Horses are supposed to eat grass. Surely a little can't hurt."

A muscle jumped along the side of Darcy's jaw line. "Most horses," she said patiently. "Not this one. If you want your daughter to be able to ride, he needs to be on a dry lot, with hay."

Muttering under his breath, the man grabbed the pony's lead rope and marched him to the back end of the horse trailer, where the pony obediently hopped inside.

"Marilyn is at the front desk and can give you a tube of bute for pain relief." Darcy watched him shut the gate. "If he isn't better within a week or two, give me a call."

"I never should have bought him in the first place. Big mistake."

"This little guy is a wonderful child's pony," Darcy said patiently. "He's a rare find with his personality and show experience. He's well worth any amount of extra care."

"Maybe you should buy him, then. I've just about had it with this whole business. I'd sell him to you cheap."

"Dad," Anna wailed, "Pepper is my best friend and—"

"Hurry inside and get that tube of bute," her father growled. "Then get in the car, Anna. We'll discuss this later."

Darcy exchanged weary glances with Kaycee after the truck and horse trailer pulled out onto the road and disappeared.

"Some people are so mean. I wouldn't want to be poor Anna," Kaycee muttered. "I think she's about to lose her buddy."

"Her dad isn't mean," Darcy said. "Not really. He

just doesn't know anything about horses, and for all we know, maybe he can't really afford to be giving his daughter this opportunity."

"Yeah, well, I still wish the pony *and* Anna luck." Kaycee glanced at her watch. "Oops—I'd better see if your eleven-o'clock client is in the waiting room."

Logan followed Darcy through the back door of the clinic. "You did a good job with that exam and the client. I'm impressed."

She lifted a shoulder in a slight shrug. "Nothing too difficult."

Curious, he leaned his good shoulder against the door frame when she stopped at the sink in the lab to wash her hands. "I thought you'd done just small-animal work."

"No. I worked in a mixed practice before coming here." She pulled her lab coat on over her scrubs. "Plus I had horses when I was a kid and did quite a bit of showing until vet school, so at one time I even thought I'd go straight equine."

"Why didn't you?"

"Well, things don't always work out the way you expect." She hesitated. Looked away. "When I inherited my aunt's house, I was grateful to find a job in town, no matter what kind of practice it was—especially since Dr. Boyd was such a great guy."

"But it sounded like you've dealt with Pepper before."

"Yeah. Boyd was okay with me seeing horses if I wanted to. But when he got sick I had to take over the clinic, so I was too busy to pursue it. What little I've done has been more of a favor to the locals, really."

She cocked her head and lifted her gaze to his. "I'm

sure you'll do very well here, but as you've now seen, there's also a strong demand for the small-animal side. So I just don't get it. You're throwing away a successful, established side of this practice if you don't let it continue."

He didn't answer. But she was right, of course. She always had been. He'd known that before ever arriving in town.

But keeping on an extra vet had never been part of his goals. She didn't fit in his plans, and he only had to recall the situation in Montana to remind him why.

Try as he might to avoid it, Darcy was already slipping through his defenses. And where would he be then? Even though she didn't seem to be anything like Cathy, would he be second-guessing every move, every billing statement? Every country vet call that might be anything but?

"Okay, then," she continued coolly into the lengthening silence between them. "Fine. But just so you know, I've started looking into possible sites in town for my own clinic. I can't afford to delay if I'm going to be without a job, so sometime soon we need to sit down and talk before I sign a lease somewhere else."

Emma pushed aside her dinner plate and craned her neck to see Darcy's laptop screen. "That looks like an ice cream truck, Mommy."

Darcy laughed and gave her a quick hug, then scrolled through the next dozen photos in the online listing. "I guess you're right. But it's actually a mobile vet clinic."

Emma gave her a baffled look.

"See the door in back? People can walk inside with their pets to see the veterinarian."

"Dogs go in there?"

"Absolutely. People, too. I could drive it around the county and see clients in different towns. Or just park it here in Aspen Creek."

Emma eyes flashed with sudden fear. "I don't want you to go far away. Not like Daddy."

"Don't worry, sweetheart, I'm not going anywhere. I'd be home every single night."

A tear traced down Emma's cheek. "Daddy said he'd be back."

Yes, he had, but trust and honor hadn't meant much to him, and he'd ultimately paid the price for it, rest his soul. And the one still suffering for his selfishness was his little girl.

"Well, I've also been looking into some empty storefronts on Main Street, and maybe that would work out better. You and I might start looking at some of them on Saturday. But right now, I need to get back to working on my bedroom floor."

"Can I help?"

"Um…no. But you can watch a DVD here in the kitchen if you want. You choose. When it's over it'll be time for your bath and storybooks."

Darcy had damp-mopped the bedroom when she first got home from work to give it time to dry fully. Now, after a painstaking hour of rubbing stain onto the hardwood floor and wiping off the excess with a dry rag, she rocked back on her heels and studied the results as she peeled off her gloves.

"You're doing a great job."

At the sound of Logan's deep voice behind her, she spun around, startled. "I didn't hear you come in."

"I had to come back into town this evening and thought I'd stop in."

Darcy blinked in disbelief. She was never careless anymore. Not ever. One lesson had been more than enough. "Did I leave the front door unlocked?"

"No. Emma saw me through the front window and opened the door. She said you were 'finger-painting' your bedroom and that I should take a look."

She laughed. "She must not think I'm very creative. It's all one color."

"Looks great, though."

"I read that medium tones would hide scuffs better than dark. I hope that's true." She studied the floor. "Next I need to apply sealer, buff it and add the polyurethane."

"I should be able to help by the weekend."

She snorted. "I don't expect that at all. Not for weeks. That shoulder still looks too painful."

"It's a lot better already."

"Right," she drawled. "Except that it's been only twenty-four hours. I see you flinch when you move it."

"That's just your imagination."

The twinkle in his eyes caught her unawares, and she glanced up at him in surprise. This wasn't the cold, distant stranger who'd shown up several weeks ago, and if she wasn't careful, she was going to start liking him a little too much.

Jerking her wayward thoughts back into line, she tapped the lid onto the empty can of stain and rose to her feet. "I figure I can put the furniture back in this room by Wednesday or Thursday, then start on Emma's room. The way it's going, I might get all of the floors done in a few weeks."

"I hope the kitchen flooring isn't a surprise. They can

sure be a bear to take out. In the meantime, I brought you something to look at."

She belatedly realized that he was holding out some sort of catalog. She accepted it and studied the cover, suppressing the surprising sensation that raced up her arm at the inadvertent brush of their fingertips.

"These are…um…cabinets?"

"The resurfacing materials I told you about. Veneers for exposed cabinet sides, new doors, drawer fronts, hardware."

After days of mulling her options, she'd decided she was staying in Aspen Creek no matter what. But if she needed to establish her own clinic, she and Emma might end up in this little cottage for a long time to come. "These things aren't cheap or flimsy, right?"

"A friend of mine totally remodeled his home and used this company. The results were stunning. He chose the top of the line, though."

"So you just nail these pieces into place? I could probably do it myself, then, while that shoulder of yours is healing."

He shot her an amused look. "It might be just a little harder than that."

The laughter in his voice felt like dark velvet sliding over her skin and made her feel warm and shivery.

And for the first time since Dean left her, she found herself wondering what it might be like to be enfolded in another man's arms once again. Maybe even lose herself in a kiss…

But she had no business even thinking about that. Not with anyone. Emma, her career and a stable, secure home were all that mattered now.

Chapter Eight

On Tuesday, ibuprofen throughout the day helped Logan see several horses that were brought into the clinic, though toward the end of the day, his shoulder was even more painful and he just wanted to get in his truck and go home

But Darcy was right. There was one thing he couldn't put off any longer. At five, he asked the staff to come into his office.

Marilyn edged in, her face pale. Kaycee fiddled with her necklace and didn't meet his eyes. But when Darcy trailed in after the others, she leaned against the wall, folded her arms and stared him down, clearly challenging him to do the right thing.

He just hoped what he'd decided *was* the right thing. "As you know, I bought this clinic planning to change the focus, update the building and search for staff experienced in an equine practice." He looked at each of them in turn. "I have reasons—good ones—for wanting to start fresh by interviewing and hiring new employees. It's a common approach in situations like this one."

If anything, Marilyn grew even more pale. Darcy reached over and rested a hand on one of hers.

Logan drew in a slow breath. "Some new owners let the previous staff interview, as well, and then make their decisions. That seems fair enough, but I don't think it's necessary here."

Kaycee scowled. "So here it comes."

"I've been here two and a half weeks now," Logan continued. "I've had time to see your efficiency and rapport with the clients, Marilyn. And Kaycee, you've done a great job with the horses and owners who've been in this week. I feel we'll all make a good team. How do you feel about working for me?"

Marilyn and Kaycee nodded, the relief in the room palpable.

Marilyn pressed a hand to her chest. "B-but what about Darcy?"

"She and I need to talk further." He looked down at a document on the desk. "One last thing. I need to have background checks done on anyone who works here— to safeguard our clients, staff and the reputation of the clinic. And that will include all of you."

After the last scheduled client was seen and Logan had left for the day, Kaycee stormed into the lab.

Darcy looked up from the X-rays she was reviewing of a dachshund with back pain. "What's up?"

"The more I think about it, the more I can't believe it," she fumed. "Background checks. Like we're criminals or something. I've been here for over two years and Marilyn for twenty. Not only that, but we've both lived here all our lives. What in the world does he think he'd going to find on us?"

"Nothing, I'm sure. And he probably knows it." Darcy turned off the light in the viewing box and tucked the films into a folder.

"It's just plain humiliating. Do I have the choice to say no?"

"If you did, you probably wouldn't have a job."

Kaycee's mouth pursed into a belligerent pout. "Maybe I don't even want it."

"Whoa, Kaycee, Think about what you're saying. Would you give up your good-paying job over this?"

"I just think it's wrong," she retorted.

"He's setting a wise policy. Can you imagine the flack if he inadvertently hired someone in the future who was on a sex offender registry? Or who had some other criminal record? Imagine the risk—and the liability he could face if something bad happened later on."

"I'll bet he isn't so perfect, either. I wonder what's in his background?"

At hearing the anger in Kaycee's voice, realization dawned. "Are you worried about…something in particular?"

Kaycee's eyes glistened with sudden tears.

"Honey, I don't know your whole story, and it's not my business. But I do know you're raising your brother and sister, so things must have been tough. You're an amazing young woman to have taken on such responsibility at…were you nineteen?"

"Almost." Kaycee gave a single short nod and looked away. "I…did a few things when I was a teenager. Bad things."

"I can help you find a lawyer if you want to be sure, but I doubt very much that any minor juvenile offenses were transferred when you became an adult. I imagine the documents were sealed."

"I don't have money for a lawyer," Kaycee retorted bitterly. "Especially not now."

"If you want, I can ask around for some advice—without mentioning your name, of course. Maybe you wouldn't even need to see a lawyer, unless there are problems with your records that need to be corrected. You could probably just start at the courthouse and ask someone in the juvenile office."

She shuddered. "Like that wouldn't be totally humiliating. It's a small town, and I know most of the people there."

"If you want, I could go with you. I can't imagine you capable of doing anything seriously wrong, though. And I don't think anyone could fault you for whatever happened in your past."

"But then there are m-my parents…" Kaycee bit her lower lip. "You know they're in prison, right? What does that say about me?"

"Their transgressions are part of their records, not yours." Darcy slid an arm around her shoulders and gave her a hug. "And I think you've become a far stronger person because of it. I would be very proud if my daughter grew up to be someone like you."

"Do you think I should just go ahead and tell Dr. Maxwell everything? I mean, would it be better if he heard it from me?"

"If you think he's going to hear things around town about your family, it might be more straightforward to get it all out in the open, so he hears the truth and not some exaggeration. But that's completely up to you."

* * *

The answering service called at two a.m. to announce crisply that a client had an emergency and was requesting immediate help.

Logan flicked on the lamp, reached for a notebook on the bedside table and jotted down the address and phone number, ignoring the pain shooting down his right arm with every movement. He groaned and eased back into bed for a few seconds, considering his options.

There was no other equine vet within forty miles. He needed to take this call. But how was he going to manage a potentially complex case given his damaged shoulder?

At the multi-vet clinic in Montana, there had been plenty of staff. Vets were on a rotating schedule for after-hours emergency farm calls, as were the vet techs who were willing and able to leave home on short notice at night if a vet needed extra help.

Here, he could set up an alternating on-call schedule with Darcy, but she was a single parent with a young child, so how would that work? And the possibility of extra help on night calls didn't look promising, either.

Kaycee had younger siblings who lived with her, and Marilyn was office help, not trained as a vet tech. She would mostly be in the way, if she tried to help with a complicated case. Unless...

Glancing at the clock, he muttered "Forgive me" as he dialed Marilyn's cell. Then he called Darcy.

Twenty minutes later, Marilyn had arrived at Darcy's place to watch over Emma as she slept, and Darcy arrived at the clinic to ride with him to the farm.

"Double-time pay, huh?" Darcy said. "Marilyn could certainly use it."

"I just felt guilty about waking her up and grateful when she said yes."

He headed for the front driver's side door, but Darcy beat him to it. "No problem, but I'm driving so you can rest that shoulder."

The main highway was empty this time of night, the headlights cutting a narrow swath of light through the pitch-black countryside. Logan typed the address into the dashboard GPS screen. A crisp female voice directed them well out of town, then onto a maze of narrow gravel roads.

"I never would've found this place without a GPS," Darcy muttered.

The final turn took them down a narrow drive to a white ranch house and a metal barn. A woman emerged from the barn and waited anxiously as Darcy grabbed the plastic tote of supplies from the backseat of the truck.

"She's in here. Please hurry."

Bright banks of fluorescent lights illuminated box stalls flanking both sides of the wide aisle in the horse barn.

A big paint mare stood cross-tied in a large cemented area with rubber mats on the floor. A water hose snaked across the wet cement.

Blood had pooled on the floor by her front hooves. The gaping wound on the bulging muscle of her forearm was least ten centimeters wide and looked deep.

"I'm Dr. Maxwell," Logan said, offering his hand. "And this is Dr. Leighton."

"Margie Ford. We raise show paints here, and Buttons is one of our best mares. I heard a ruckus outside and found her fighting with a horse in the next corral.

Two of the fence boards were splintered, so I think she ran into the sharp edges. It was bleeding pretty good at first, but I applied pressure for about twenty minutes. Now it's just seeping a little."

Logan leaned close and studied the damage, then listened to the mare's heart and lung sounds. "Has she been bred for next year?"

"We thought so, but she came back into heat yesterday."

"I need to sedate her to examine this. We need to determine just how extensive it is."

Margie nodded. "Absolutely."

Darcy drew a dose of xylazine into a syringe and handed it to him. He palpated the neck, found the jugular vein and, after temporarily occluding the flow of blood with his thumb, delivered the sedative.

The mare stood patiently through it all. As soon as her muzzle began to droop toward the floor, he donned surgical gloves and began gently probing the wound with his fingertips. "Did you remove any wood splinters?"

"I didn't see any, and didn't want to poke around in there to find out. I did start to rinse it off with the hose but figured it was better to leave that to you."

"Good. Sterile saline is better." He gritted his teeth as a wave of pain seared through his shoulder. "Darcy? If you could take over, that would be great."

"Got it." She donned surgical gloves, grabbed an IV bag of the saline from the tote and filled a syringe, then removed the needle. Using the syringe as a gentle water pistol, she began gently flushing dirt and debris from the wound.

After refilling the syringe a half-dozen times, she

set it aside and began probing the wound, checking its depth and feeling for foreign objects.

Every movement was gentle and sure, and she was exceptionally thorough. Logan relaxed as his confidence in her clinical skills grew.

Darcy looked up at Margie. "Fortunately, most of this is shallow. There's a central depth of around seven centimeters, though."

Margie moved closer and anxiously peered into the wound. "But she'll be all right? No major damage?"

"The bone wasn't compromised, so that's very good news. Now we just need to keep the wound clean and let it heal." Darcy reached for an autoclave bag, pulled out sterilized surgical scissors and trimmed away several dangling tags of shredded hide. "These small bits will die and just impede healing. It's best to clean up the edges of the wound."

"You're not going to stitch it all up?" Margie asked in disbelief. "Won't this leave a massive scar?"

"It looks bad to you now, but I don't think it will. I'd like to suture just the upper half of the wound and leave the lower five centimeters open for drainage." Darcy glanced up at Logan. "Dr. Maxwell?"

He nodded. "I agree."

"I'm going to give her a strong antibiotic today by injection and leave you with Bactrim tablets you can dissolve in water and give her twice a day starting tomorrow night." Darcy looked over at Margie. "Can you handle that?"

"Of course. No problem."

"It's a tricky place to bandage, given the tapering of the foreleg toward the knee," Darcy continued. "But I'd still like to wrap it for tonight and tomorrow to keep it clean, then come back tomorrow late afternoon to irrigate the wound and see how it's doing. After that we'll look at a progression of different types of dressings, depending on the stage of wound healing."

Darcy rifled through the tote at her feet and applied a dressing held by a thin layer of cotton wrap, followed by fluffy roll cotton and a cohesive elastic wrap over it all. "Done. But give us a call if the bandage slips, and one of us can come back to replace it."

"I'm so glad you two were able to come. It's great knowing that we've actually got equine vets in the area again." Margie blew out a relieved breath. "I'll be calling you from now on."

"Thanks, ma'am." Logan touched the brim of his hat as he and Darcy sauntered out into the darkness toward his truck.

Out here, so far from the lights of town, the sky was awash with glittering stars. It was chilly during the pre-dawn hours, and he saw Darcy shiver.

He casually dropped his good arm around her shoulders as they walked. It was just a friendly gesture to share warmth, but he felt her tense, and he dropped his arm.

Interesting.

She'd felt so…right, nestled within that hug. He hadn't wanted to let her go. Somehow his thoughts had instantly conjured up images of long evenings over coffee. Candlelit dinners. She'd clearly felt anything but.

He had yet to hear anyone mention her boyfriend, spouse or partner, yet what was such a lovely, sweet and hardworking person like her doing all alone? There must have been someone, because she had a daughter… but where was he?

What if he'd been abusive?

A surge of protectiveness rushed through Logan at the thought, though a small voice whispered that her life was none of his business. He sat at an angle on the passenger side of the truck and casually watched her as she drove back to Aspen Creek.

Bluish smudges of exhaustion left dark circles under her eyes, but she was smiling to herself and humming a faint song completely out of tune.

Nope, it definitely was none of his business.

And yet he found himself clearing his throat. "You did a fine job out there."

She shot a quick glance at him. "Thanks, but it wasn't much, really."

"But it was. That suturing was done perfectly, and you didn't make a move that a top-notch vet wouldn't have made. So now I'm even more curious. You have real talent for the equine side of things. Why did you leave it behind?"

"It's a long story." Her jaw hardened and she gripped the steering wheel until her knuckles whitened. "And not all that interesting."

But he guessed it was.

In the dark intimacy of the truck cab, illuminated only by the dashboard lights, he felt emboldened enough to step over the bounds she'd clearly set…curious if the mystery surrounding her was somehow tied to her troublesome financial situation.

"Is it a secret?" he teased.

She rolled her eyes. "Not really. I can promise you my worst legal transgressions have been a few speeding tickets, and I didn't leave the previous practice under any sort of cloud. I enjoyed the work. I liked the clinic.

But it was simply time to move on, so I did. Without regrets. Now Aspen Creek has become our home, with good friends, a great church and clientele at the clinic whom I enjoy very much."

It was an answer…and yet it wasn't.

He belatedly realized that he'd opened himself up to the same question, but she didn't ask the obvious. Instead, she settled into a comfortable silence. Dawn was brightening the eastern sky in ribbons of gold and mauve when she pulled up at the clinic next to her car.

Leaving the truck motor running, she glanced at the digital clock on the dashboard and climbed out of the cab.

"See you back here in a couple hours," she said with a wry smile. "Have a good night's sleep."

He watched her car pull out of the parking lot, its taillights glowing like rubies as it disappeared down the street.

He'd asked a simple, reasonable question about her past and she'd shut down like a door clanging shut on a bank vault…but not before he'd seen a flash of vulnerability in her eyes.

And now he had more questions than ever before.

Chapter Nine

Wednesday passed in a blur, what with a busy clinic schedule and another trip out to Margie's place with Logan to check on the paint mare.

When Darcy finally picked up Emma at the sitter's and got home, she was too tired to make anything more than hamburgers and green beans for supper.

But afterward, once Emma was tucked into bed, she finished the final coat of polyurethane on the master bedroom floor, flopped onto the sofa—the only piece of furniture in the living room—and heaved a sigh of relief. One room done.

She'd been flippant while telling Logan she could do it all herself once it was clear that he'd be laid up for a while. Saving his time for more complex projects had seemed logical at the time.

True, she could follow directions and slowly get the floors done, but all of the steps took more time than she'd dreamed. And after prying at the vinyl on the kitchen floor for an hour, she knew it was going to be one of the most difficult things she'd ever done.

At a knock on the door she jumped, startled and a

little nervous as always about a stranger showing up on her porch after dark. Her heart had been broken after losing her elderly dog Elsie last fall, but as a single parent, Darcy also missed her fierce barking whenever someone approached the house.

No stranger would have guessed the noisy dog inside was a thirty-pound marshmallow.

"Yoo-hoo, are you home?" At the sound of Beth's cheerful voice, Darcy hurried to the front door and let her in.

"I have to follow up on everyone who won a handyman at the auction and make sure things are working out." Her arm curved around a clipboard, Beth surveyed the furniture piled in the kitchen and the bare floor of the living room. "Wow. You're sure making progress. Is Logan working out for you?"

"Very well. He repaired the picket fence and also started the flooring, but then injured his shoulder. He also has some great ideas for the kitchen cupboards, though there might not be enough hours to cover any of that."

"And how are you two getting along?" Beth waggled her eyebrows. "I was just at the salon getting my hair trimmed, and he seemed to be the hot topic of the day. Sooo handsome. So nice. So eligible. Just thought I'd mention it in case you've had any thoughts in that direction."

"No. Absolutely not. It can be open season on Dr. Maxwell for as long as it takes for someone to tie him down. Really."

Beth gave her a speculative look, her mouth twitching. "Sounds like an awful lot of protest."

"Well, I mean it. You know what happened back in

Minnesota with Dean. I *trusted* him. How can I dare fall for anyone else and be sure it won't happen again? I was completely clueless." Darcy snorted. "As in, too stupid to live."

"I predict you're going to find the right guy someday. A guy you can completely trust and love forever. And then you'll have to eat your words. For the record, I do think your new vet is pretty hot."

Well…yes. And he was turning out to be a much nicer guy than she'd first thought. But that didn't mean she would take a chance on him or anyone else. "It just isn't worth it. And what about Emma? I don't want to start dating and have her thinking she'll have a new daddy soon, then be heartbroken if the relationship doesn't work out. She is my priority."

"How is she doing, by the way? I heard she had an asthma episode after church last Sunday, when my husband and I were out of town."

"She was fine after using her rescue inhaler. This time of year is tough for her, with the grasses and weeds, but molds and perfumes spell trouble, too. Since there were a lot of visitors at church for a baptism, maybe it was perfume."

"Poor sweetheart."

"She's been fine since. We just never know. Sometime she even starts wheezing without any of her usual triggers nearby. The doctor said her sensitivities could change over time. I'm just hoping they go away."

"Me, too. It's always a worry having something like that. By the way—different topic—we've missed you at the book club lately. Monday mornings, eight o'clock at my bookstore?" Beth teased. "Thought I would mention it since we haven't seen you for so long."

"I used to keep that first hour on Monday morning open so I could join you, but things have been a lot busier lately. Once we get into summer and people are traveling, the schedule at the clinic will slow down."

Beth gave her a knowing look. "When you come, bring that vet you're definitely not interested in. We have some new members who might like to check him out."

Check him out, indeed. Beth's words kept slipping into Darcy's thoughts as she worked through a busy appointment schedule the next day. How did she feel about that, really?

She'd told Beth the truth. She wasn't looking for a relationship. Dean had pretty much cured her of that basic human longing for companionship and love. She'd had to immerse herself in prayer to finally let go of the hurt and anger following his betrayal.

But did she really want to see Logan madly in love with someone else? It was selfish not to wish him happiness. She didn't even know him that well.

But with every day that she worked with him, with every conversation, she'd started to see new sides to him that had begun to touch her heart.

With several emergency call-ins and no extra time in her schedule to cover them, he had taken the extra appointments this afternoon so those clients wouldn't face long waits.

Now, on her way to the lab, she passed the open door of an exam room where an elderly woman hovered anxiously over her obese Maltese while Logan checked its heart and lung sounds.

It was Mrs. Peabody, dressed as usual in her faded

print Sunday dress, sturdy laced shoes and a sagging sweater that had seen better days. Bent over and always short of breath, she religiously brought her dog into the clinic for the slightest signs or symptoms but was only able to pay a few dollars each time against her ever-growing account.

Darcy hated to accept even that much from her and had begun charging her less and less, waving off the old woman's protests by saying, "Today we're having a sale," or "I really didn't do that much, anyway."

Darcy lingered just past the door, hoping Logan wouldn't look at Mrs. Peabody's balance at the top of the clinic visit sheet. Hoping he wouldn't say anything less than tactful. If she asked about today's cost and he told her the truth, she'd probably succumb to a massive heart attack at his feet.

"I-is my baby all right?" The old woman's voice quavered. "I was so afraid this morning when his breathing didn't sound right. H-he's all I have left, doctor."

It was true. Her husband had died years ago, and her only child—a retired teacher—had passed back in December. Without her little companion, by now the crushing loneliness and grief might have taken Mrs. Peabody, as well.

There was a long pause. Darcy held her breath.

"He's a beautiful dog, ma'am. And don't you worry. His heart and lungs sound fine. There's one thing he needs to do, though."

"I suppose you want him to lose weight," she said on a long sigh. "Dr. Leighton says that, too. But he gets exactly the right amount of dog food."

"The weight loss formula?"

She nodded. "What Dr. Leighton prescribed. I buy it here."

"Then it's the extra little treats that have to go. Being overweight is very hard on his heart, so he needs less food and more walking."

Darcy continued on to the lab, the voices following her down the hall.

"But he loves his treats and looks at me so sadly if he doesn't get just a tiny bit off my plate," she said sorrowfully. "How can I refuse? What is life without small pleasures?"

Darcy smiled to herself, waiting for his response. *Good luck, Dr. Logan.*

Footsteps came down the hall, and Logan appeared at the door of the lab. "Do we have any sample-size bags of light dog treats?"

"Top shelf, on your left. But—"

He grabbed a couple of bags and left before she could warn him about billing Mrs. Peabody.

His voice filtered down the hall as he explained the low-calorie treats and a proper diet.

Darcy once again held her breath when she heard him wrapping up his advice and saying farewell.

Then warmth washed over her like a gentle hug as she heard his next words.

"No—of course not." His voice dropped to a conspiratorial whisper that Darcy could barely hear. "No charge for today. We weren't that busy, and I didn't really do anything. Anyway, we all love to see you and your beautiful little dog."

After dialing the front desk and telling Marilyn there'd be no charge for the elderly lady toddling slowly down the hall with her dog, Logan left the exam room to head to back to his office.

As he passed the lab, Darcy stepped out the door and they nearly collided. He grasped both of her upper arms when she staggered, but quickly released her.

Her eyes widened. "Sorry."

He said it at the same moment she did, and they both laughed self-consciously as they stepped back. The air between them seemed to quiver with emotion and un-spoken possibilities.

She readjusted the stethoscope draped around her neck. "How was Mrs. Peabody's dog?"

"Obese."

"She worries about him all the time, you know. He's the only friend she has. Her family is gone, and I hear all of her human friends have passed on, as well. Um… I couldn't help overhearing…" She angled an amused smile at him. "If you talk loud enough for her to hear, you might as well be using a loudspeaker. Sounds like you charged her as much as I do."

He felt himself flush a little. "This can't be run as a free clinic, but…"

"I know. You don't have to say it. She's just such a sweet old lady." Her eyes twinkled with silent laughter as her soft gaze locked on his and a faint blush stained her cheekbones. "I'm just relieved to find you have the same soft side for her that I do. And about those light treats? Tried already. The next time she came in, she told me he didn't like them—unless she slathered them with gravy. But I'm sure she didn't want to admit that to you."

"A losing battle?"

"Definitely a losing battle. She loves him up with

food, and after seeing that dog for a year, I can tell you that it isn't going to change."

The equine practice back in Montana had been highly professional. Successful. Busy. A well-run business—at least, until Cathy showed up. But from his first day in Aspen Creek, this town, these people and this practice had been proving to be so much more. Quirky. Warm. Populated with people who really seemed to care about each other.

"Does she truly understand how serious this is?" he asked. "Her little buddy isn't going to have a very long life if he doesn't lose weight."

"I figure it's like water dripping on a stone. If we talk to her every time she comes in, we may finally wear her down. I just hope it isn't too late." Darcy eyed him thoughtfully. "I'm guessing that this sort of thing wasn't an issue at your last practice."

He had to laugh at that. "Not often. But then, we weren't dealing with doting small-animal owners like Mrs. Peabody. Our clients included most of the large breeding farms in the county. A lot of training facilities and many of the smaller show stables. Anyone who wasn't concerned about optimal feeding and health care wouldn't stay in business very long."

"Do you miss it?"

"The practice?" He considered that for a moment. "I miss...what it was. The state-of-the-art, high-tech equipment that made it easier to provide the very best of care. Much of it is beyond the financial reach of a one- or two-vet practice. I miss the large staff."

"But things changed."

"Yeah. Some things changed." He lifted his uninjured shoulder dismissively. "So now I'm glad to be where I am. Where ideally I have more control if issues arise."

"Except with the Mrs. Peabodys of the world?" she teased.

"I have to believe that she'll eventually listen to reason. I'm not giving up on her."

"Good luck with that." Darcy patted his arm. "You keep trying, and I'll start praying. And sooner or later, it's gonna happen. He cares for the least of his creatures, you know."

He watched her head down the hall to an exam room, where another client was waiting.

Praying.

She'd said the word with such simple, straightforward faith. No hint of doubt, no hesitance about the power of prayer.

He knew the exact date when he'd last hoped prayer could alter the course of his life, and God hadn't been listening that time, either. Logan hadn't sent any more desperate pleas heavenward after that. But now he began to wonder. Was it ever possible to regain a child-like faith after so many things had gone wrong?

Chapter Ten

Kaycee peered out of the kennel room in back and motioned to Darcy. "Could I talk to you for a minute?"

She closed the door after Darcy stepped inside. "I've been thinking about what you said."

"About…"

"About what might show up on a background check. Or surface because of some old…um…gossip."

"I see."

"Dr. Boyd knew everything and he was so nice about it. But now I wonder whether or not I should go ahead and tell Dr. Maxwell. Before he gets that background check done, I mean."

"And what did you decide?"

"I guess…well, maybe you're right. If I don't say anything and he finds out, maybe he'll think I was trying to hide all the bad stuff. Or that I can't be trusted. But I can't just go up to him out of the blue. That would be so weird, you know?"

"So…what do you want me to do?"

"I…um…wonder if you could come in with me. You know, like having someone in my corner?"

"Moral support."

Her mouth twisted. "It still makes me mad, having to do this. If you live in a glass house you shouldn't throw stones, right?"

"What?"

Kaycee shifted uncomfortably and looked away.

"Kaycee?"

"Just something I found out about him on Google. It doesn't matter. I'm just really afraid I'll mess this up. And if I do and he fires me, what am I gonna do?"

"Do you want to catch him right now before he leaves for home?"

"No." Kaycee's eyes rounded. "Well…maybe. Yes. If I think about this too much longer, I'm going to be sick."

Logan looked up from his computer screen in obvious surprise when Kaycee and Darcy walked in his office door. "Is something wrong?"

Kaycee plopped into one of the chairs in front of the desk and mutely looked down at her hands, suddenly looking far younger than her twenty-three years.

Darcy took the other chair and waited for the girl to speak. After a long, awkward moment of silence, she turned to Logan. "Kaycee needs her job very much. But she's concerned about some things in her past and wants to be up front with you."

Logan's gaze softened with understanding as he shifted his focus to Kaycee. "If this is about the background checks, I got that information today, and they were perfectly fine for all three of you. I fully expected they would be, by the way. I hope you weren't too upset about having it done, but…well, I've been in situations in which more care would've saved people a lot of grief."

Kaycee lifted her gaze to meet his, her eyes hard and narrowed. Then she looked away. "I can imagine."

Logan tilted his head and frowned as he studied her for a moment, then he leaned back, his elbows on the arms of his chair and his fingertips steepled. "Is there anything you wanted to discuss?"

Mystified by the uneasy currents of emotion in the room, Darcy glanced between them. "Kaycee?"

The girl closed her eyes as she drew in a deep breath. "Okay. Just in case you were to hear gossip around town, I wanted you to hear everything from me first. My parents abused and dealt drugs for years, so I pretty much raised my brother and sister ever since I was in middle school. I…um…got caught shoplifting at the grocery store a couple times. But I had to try, 'cause there wasn't any money and sometimes we had nothing to eat."

"I'm sorry you had to go through that," Logan said gently.

"It's better now." Kaycee's voice took on a belligerent edge. "The kids live with me, they're on Badger Care state insurance, and the state helps out now that Mom and Dad are in prison. We're doing just fine." She launched to her feet as if ready to flee. "I promise that I'm trustworthy and I'll work hard. I *need* this job more than you could know."

An easy smile on his face, Logan stood and offered his hand to her across the desk. "Then it sounds like we have a perfect deal, because I need you, too. I'm glad to have you on board."

"That took some courage," Darcy said quietly after Kaycee left. "She's one of the strongest kids I've ever met. What a relief to hear that her background check was clear."

"It wasn't, actually."

"What?" Darcy leaned back in her chair, aghast. "But you told her it was."

"I told her it was *fine*, and I meant it. When I asked the sheriff to run criminal background checks, he said he couldn't help me much because Kaycee's juvenile records were sealed. But Marilyn stopped me after work one day, and said she wanted me to know the truth in case someone gossiped about Kaycee later on."

"Oh."

"That poor kid has had a real struggle raising her siblings, but even as a teen she fought to keep them out of foster care and together. How many kids her age would've taken on that responsibility?"

"Not many could have handled it. That's for sure."

"From all accounts, she's done a fine job ever since. She keeps them clean and well fed, they never miss school or activities, and she helps with homework. There are many parents who don't do half as well. I'm impressed, and I need employees like her."

Warmth and relief settled around Darcy's heart. "That's just about the kindest thing I've heard in a very long time. A lot of people would take one look at her past, assume she could be a risk and just let her go."

"Then they would be wrong. Her parents aren't going to be out on the street for thirty years, and before being incarcerated, they were guilty of abuse and neglect. So how could I not give her every chance to succeed?"

Darcy wanted to reach across the desk and kiss him in heartfelt thanks for his quiet compassion. And then kiss him again for his kindness in helping Kaycee hang onto her pride during what had to have been a terrifying confession.

"That's exactly how I feel." Her gaze locked on his. She felt her pulse escalate as she rose and took a careful step back lest she find herself impulsively giving in to that temptation. "I realize I've misjudged you, Logan. Thank you from the bottom of my heart."

Saturday morning dawned bright and sunny, with the promise of clear skies and seventy degrees throughout the day.

It was a perfect day for opening all the windows in the little house and tackling the floor in Emma's room. But it was also perfect for making good on her promise, and that promise had to be kept.

So after the clinic closed at noon, she picked up Emma at the babysitter's house, took her home for lunch, then got ready to leave again.

"Are you ready to go?" Darcy helped Emma into a pink sweater with kittens and puppies embroidered on the front. "Hannah is waiting for us."

Emma fidgeted while Darcy fastened her buttons. "I want to go *now*. Please? What if there aren't any puppies left?"

"There will be, I promise. Remember all the photos we looked at last night on the rescue website?"

"They were every color. Puppies and big dogs, too."

Darcy smiled and gave her a hug. "Have you decided which ones are your favorites?"

The little girl frowned. "I can't remember."

"Well, we'll take lots of time. If you can't decide, we can always go back again."

They walked out to the car and Darcy buckled her

into the booster seat, then got behind the wheel and turned the key in the ignition. At the *click-click-click* sound she dropped her head against the headrest and groaned.

"What's wrong, Mommy?"

"It won't start."

"But what about the puppies?" Her voice rose to a wail. "You promised!"

"Well, we might—"

At the distinctive sound of Logan's diesel pickup pulling into the driveway, Darcy glanced in the rear-view mirror. *Good timing, buddy.*

She climbed out of her car and met him halfway. He held out his hand, and she blinked in surprise at her cell phone. "Oh, my— I thought it was in my purse."

"Marilyn noticed it at the clinic, but she was heading for Minneapolis for the weekend, so I said I could drop it by."

"Many, many thanks. We don't have a landline, so I wouldn't have missed it until I tried calling AAA road service."

He looked over her shoulder. "What's wrong with the car?"

"Won't start. It's doing a clickety-click thing when I turn the key in the ignition, and Emma is pretty upset." She turned to help the child out of her booster seat. "I bought a new battery two months ago, so I'm guessing it's the starter."

"Mommy said we could get a puppy today, and now we can't," Emma said sadly. Her face brightened when her gaze veered past Logan to his truck. "Maybe you could come! Will your car go?"

"That's a pickup, honey. And no, we don't need to bother Dr. Maxwell. I'm sure he's very busy."

"Actually, I'd like a good excuse to not go home." He sauntered to her car and tried the ignition. "I'd guess the starter, as well. Do you have a good mechanic?"

"Red's seems to be good. So, why don't you want to go home?"

"This is the weekend I'm finally dealing with all of the unpacked moving boxes still stacked in the house. I can't stand looking at them any longer, and I might have company coming next weekend."

Company?

Maybe a girlfriend from Montana?

Of course he would still have relationships with people back there. Maybe really close ones. It shouldn't have been any surprise, but she still felt a little pang in her heart.

"Should you be doing that lifting?" she asked. "What about your arm?"

He cautiously rolled his shoulder, then grinned. "It's actually pretty good. Another week and it should be fine."

Emma tugged the sleeve of Darcy's sweater and looked up at her with a pleading expression. "He *wants* to go see the puppies. Maybe he'll want one, too. Please?"

"Even if you call the road service now, there'll be no mechanics to check your car until Monday—or later. I'll get her booster seat, and we can be on our way." Logan reached into the car to grab it and put it into the backseat of his truck.

"If you do this for us, then we have to return the favor. How about we come out tomorrow afternoon to help you after church? We can even bring a picnic basket with lunch."

"You don't need to." He thought for a moment and gave her a lopsided smile. "Then again, lunch sounds mighty nice. Deal."

Her eyes twinkled. "Oops. I just remembered that I won't have a car. But I have a wonderful idea—you could come with us to church this time!"

"Uh…"

"Pastor Mark is wonderful, I promise. Every Sunday, I feel so…so renewed by his sermons. It's hard to explain, but I feel like a better person. More able to deal with everything in my life, because my faith has been uplifted. Growing up, my parents made me attend their church, and I didn't want to go. Now I really hate to miss."

She took a deep breath. "I'm sorry. I don't mean to be pushing something at you that you don't want. I should have my car fixed in a couple days, and then Emma and I can come help. We'll still owe you a return favor, after all."

He stared out into the backyard for a long moment as if sorting through his thoughts.

"I had the same upbringing you did, but…bad things happened. God and I reached an impasse when I learned that my faith really didn't help. But I'll pick you two up tomorrow and take you to church if that's what you want."

She could see he wasn't thrilled—he was simply determined to do the right thing. She barreled ahead anyway before he could change his mind. "Perfect. That's so nice of you! Emma and I will pack a lunch and come out to help you unpack, or clean, or whatever. It's the least we can do."

Emma scrambled into the truck, and he clicked the seatbelt into position. "This is sure a pretty booster," he teased, ruffling the top of her hair. "I've never seen a pink one. You must be a big girl now."

She nodded vigorously. "I'm *four*."

"Just the right age for a puppy, then."

Darcy directed him to the highway leading out of town, then up a narrow lane leading through the forest toward Hannah's house.

All the way, Logan kept up a steady patter of silly conversation with Emma that kept her laughing.

Darcy felt an ache settle in her chest at how hungry Emma seemed for male attention.

But of course she was. In time she probably wouldn't remember much about her father, but having a loving male influence in her life was something she would always miss.

Hannah's house stood at the very end of the lane. She was out in the yard and gave the truck a startled look when Logan pulled in and parked, but relaxed as they all climbed out.

"You made it," she exclaimed as she picked up Emma for a big hug. "I'm so glad. I have all sorts of little guys who are eager to meet you—and some older ones, too."

She sized up Logan with a sweeping glance and grinned. "I have just the thing for you, too."

She led the way to the backyard, probably Emma's favorite place in the whole world.

The perimeter was enclosed in high chain link fencing, with three separate large runs to the right. In back stood a new red metal barn with crisp white trim and a large enclosure with colorful chickens inside.

Emma stood on her tiptoes, looking at the far end of the yard. "Is the pony here?"

"She's probably way out in the pasture right now." Hannah reached over and gave Darcy's hand a quick squeeze. "I asked Ethan to take the kids to a matinee so there'd be a bit less commotion. But I want you to be the first to hear—he and I have set a date. The Fourth of July weekend!"

Darcy's heart filled with joy for her closest friend in Aspen Creek. "I'm so thrilled for you both. This is the best news I've had in a long, long time."

Hannah beamed. "And next week the contractor will be breaking ground on the new animal shelter in town. It's finally happening."

Darcy nodded. "Hannah and several other women in town have been managing a private, licensed animal shelter system on their own properties until enough money could be raised. They've done a wonderful job."

"And Darcy has been a great help to us, donating her free time after clinic hours and helping with the fund-raising. Once we get the facility done, we'll be able to do so much more."

"Where are the puppies?" Emma spun around to look in every direction. "Are they gone?"

Hannah led them all to the barn and ushered them inside, where the space had been divided into six large pens with pet doors leading outside to individual runs, plus areas for horse feed, dog food and supplies.

Emma rushed to the pen at the far end, where puppies were squealing and standing on their hind legs at the chain link fence, vying for attention.

"I'm grateful every single day that insurance covered the fire," Hannah said as she led Darcy and Logan down the aisle to join Emma. "The old barn wasn't big enough anyway, and this one makes our work so much easier."

The other pens held an assortment of older dogs. Some cowered at the back corners and avoided eye contact. Others bounced to the front of their pens and frantically yelped for attention.

"Oh, my," Darcy whispered, halting in front of a pen. A thin, bedraggled dog stood at the back, its head hanging low and muzzle pressed into the corner, the picture of depression and hopelessness. Heavy mats of hair hung from its body, exposing taut flesh pulled painfully tight by the twisted mats.

Logan stopped next to her and stared. "I'll never understand why people are so cruel. What's the story on this one?"

"She just came yesterday," Hannah said. "Abuse. Neglect. The neighbors who finally reported her said she was kept in a small, filthy pen and never let out—not even for a walk. From her behavior, I suspect little or no friendly human contact for ages."

"I sure hope the owners were arrested."

Hannah shook her head. "I have no idea if she even has a name, so I've been calling her Cedar. I called your office yesterday for an appointment. She'll be in Tuesday."

Logan frowned. "Let's fit her in on Monday so we can check her over. With a good clipping and bath, we can see what's under that mess."

"I had hoped we wouldn't ever see one as bad as Belle, who was dropped off last winter. But I guess I shouldn't overestimate human nature." Hannah whistled, and a gleaming chestnut-colored dog—a springer-shepherd mix—loped into the barn, its tail wagging. "This is Belle, who came to us as a surprise one night. I'm not sure who looked worse—Belle or this poor gal—but now Belle has her forever home right here."

An old, deep red golden retriever with a white muzzle limped in, its banner of a tail waving.

"And this is Maisie, who will never leave, either, right?" Darcy leaned over to give her some good rubs beneath her collar.

"Never." Hannah laughed wryly. "I really try not to adopt everything that come along, honest. But these two just stole my heart."

Down at the puppy pen, Emma held her hands flat against the chain link and shrieked with delight. "They're licking me. It tickles!"

A thin yellow lab mix in the next pen stood watching, her achingly hopeful gaze pinned on Emma, her tail wagging slowly as if she didn't quite dare to hope.

When Emma noticed, she moved in front of her pen and stared into her soulful eyes. "This one is lonely, Mommy. She's so sad."

The lab's tail moved a little faster as she pushed the black tip of her nose through the fence.

"I think she likes me. She doesn't want to be here."

"That's because she's waiting for someone to love who will love her right back for the rest of her life," Hannah said softly.

A single tear fell down Emma's cheek. "How come she doesn't have a family?"

"Some people think a puppy would be fun and cute, but have no idea how much work a puppy is...or they just lose interest. Dogs sometimes end up in a shelter if their owners get sick or pass away."

Darcy moved over to the pen and hunkered down next to Emma to take a better look. "What's the story on this one?"

"That's Bonnie. She's around three years old and had a good home, but her elderly owner died suddenly, and no one in the family was willing to take her. She was too depressed to eat for a week. She's doing better as long as I hand-feed her, so at least her ribs don't show quite as much. She came with vet records that show she's up to date on vaccinations and worming."

Emma looked up at Darcy. "This is the one, Mommy."

"I thought you wanted a playful little puppy, sweetie. You've been talking about that for a long time."

"Not anymore." Emma lifted her chin to a stubborn tilt.

"What Hannah said about dogs giving us their lifetime love is true about the puppies, too," Darcy said.

Emma's lower lip trembled. "I want this one."

Hannah smiled down at her. "Well, I'm sure your mom would want to check her over very carefully, and then you would all need to get to know each other during several visits. My first rule here is that no one can make snap decisions, because if they regret it later, the dog suffers yet another confusing, upsetting change. That's not fair."

"Can she come out now?"

"Let's see how she does. Just don't move quickly or try to grab her, okay? We need to take it easy. She's a sweet dog, but this change to a new place has been scary for her."

Hannah reached for a leash snapped to the front of

the pen and went inside. Murmuring to Bonnie, she stroked the animal's thin side and then gently scratched behind her ear.

Reassured, the dog came closer and licked Hannah's hand. "You see? She's very sweet. I understand she was a very well-mannered pet. It's just that the noise, strange dogs and unfamiliar people can be terribly intimidating."

Darcy watched as Emma edged slowly up to Hannah.

"Can I pet her?"

"Talk to her a bit first."

"You're going to be mine," Emma whispered. "And you'll be happy. You can sleep on my bed with my dollies and me."

Darcy bit back a smile as the dog extended her nose to sniff Emma's hand, and wagged her tail faster when Emma gently stroked her neck.

"She likes me, Mommy!"

"Yes, I think she does. She's probably hoping to find a new friend, just like you are." Darcy glanced over her shoulder and found Logan hunkered down in front of Cedar, the newest rescue. "What do you think—"

But he wasn't listening. He was murmuring gentle words to the ragged dog, promising all sorts of wonderful things. Toys and treats and soft beds, and the company of someone who would care for her forever. She was still at the back of her cage, but she was watching him intently. Her single, wary step in his direction was a victory.

This was yet another glimpse of a man she found more intriguing as the days and weeks passed. She'd never expected to discover a deep sense of kindness and caring in the cold, remote cowboy she'd met on that first morning he'd arrived.

And now, the evidence of his soft heart was confirmed, because it looked like Logan had just found himself a dog.

Logan slowly opened the door of the dog pen and let himself inside, then sat down in one of the front corners to appear as nonthreatening as possible.

The emaciated dog fled to the back of the pen when the door opened, as far from him as possible, and stood hunched and shaking, her tail tucked between her legs and lowered head pressed against the chain links to avoid looking at him.

His heart twisted painfully at her terrified reaction. She was expecting a beating. What kind of vicious animal of a human being could vent his rage and cruelty on a poor dog?

Even though he'd seen many similar cases of abuse over the years, just the thought of them always made him feel ill and angry and even a little helpless. How many others were never rescued? He helped whenever he could, but it broke his heart to think of any animal suffering.

And another thought always lurked in the back of his mind. If the perpetrator was this cruel and had a wife and kids, what was happening to them behind closed doors?

He began to hum softly, his gaze fixed on a distant point away from Cedar, his posture relaxed. And then he began to croon to her again, a quiet litany of praise and encouragement.

"Here—try this." Hannah opened the door of the pen

a few inches and tossed him a small plastic bag filled with dog treats. "I keep these on hand for just this sort of thing. The dogs love them."

He caught the bag. "Thanks."

"I spent quite a bit of time with her yesterday, and she finally came close enough for me to pet her, but she seems to be more wary with men. I can't wait to get started on clipping her. She'll feel so much better."

Logan tossed a dog treat midway across the pen and continued talking to the dog. "I've got more of these," he said softly. "Things are going to be so much better for you now."

He'd pursued his lifelong dream of working with horses, but on the rare free hours away from classes and labs and studying during vet school, he'd volunteered at a shelter.

This was what he'd imagined when he'd first started dreaming of vet school as a child. He'd wanted to rescue damaged animals and make them whole, and then bring them all home. It just wasn't possible to adopt them all, of course. In those childish dreams, he hadn't considered the sheer magnitude and impossibility of such a plan.

But when the dog in front of him finally dared to look his way and gave a single, tentative wave of her tail, he knew that this one had just found her forever home.

With him.

Chapter Eleven

It was yet another perfect spring day, with the sweet scent of lilacs in the air. A profusion of bright flowers along the foundation of the old church nodded in the light breeze.

Feeling as if he had his father's hand on his collar to shove him forward, Logan self-consciously followed Darcy and Emma up the steps of the white clapboard Aspen Creek Community Church.

The steeple soared toward the clouds above wide double doors that welcomed the crowd of parishioners arriving for worship.

A big crowd, he realized. Kids chasing each other on the grass, burning off energy, adults of all ages greeting each other warmly with hugs and handshakes. A number of them approached Darcy with cheerful smiles, and some even welcomed him with a masculine thump on the back, though he recognized only a few.

"Let's sit in the back," Darcy whispered as they entered the cool darkness of the church, redolent with the scents of flowers, candle wax and lemon furniture polish.

They slipped into a pew and Emma settled between them with a small felt bag of books, crayons and coloring books she'd taken from a rack as they came in.

She looked up at Logan, her troubled eyes searching his face as if she were trying to remember something important. She leaned closer. "My daddy used to come with us. But he died."

Darcy heard her, too, and reached over to take Emma's hand for a gentle squeeze.

"We gotta be quiet now," Emma whispered.

Died? The word hit him like a sucker punch to the chest, robbing him of breath.

He'd certainly known there must have been someone in Darcy's life at some point—a boyfriend, a significant other, maybe a husband. But he hadn't brought it up. He hadn't felt it was his business to pry.

Now, after coming to know this little family, he imagined the wrenching loss of someone they had loved. How it must have devastated both of them.

He felt a stab of guilt, remembering all of the doubts he'd had over Darcy's apparent financial troubles, and his worry that it might make her a liability in the office—just like his ex-fiancée.

He'd imagined careless spending. An addiction to online shopping—which had brought his spendthrift sister to the brink of bankruptcy more than once. Or maybe lavish vacations. Gambling. Jewelry, maybe—though there'd certainly been no evidence of that.

But instead of enjoying luxuries, she'd had to deal with the financial burdens of burying a young husband and perhaps years of illness before that. Starting over in Aspen Creek. Making a home for her little girl. Juggling the heavy responsibilities. Motherhood. A career.

And then there was the new owner of the clinic, who had quickly implied that she soon wouldn't even have a job.

He closed his eyes, feeling like a complete jerk, as the congregation began to sing the lyrics of a contemporary praise hymn on a large screen behind the altar.

And then a small hand slipped into his. He looked down at the concern on Emma's sweet face and felt a renewed stab of guilt.

"If you're sad about my daddy, it's okay," she whispered. "Mommy says he's dancing in heaven with the angels and my grandma. And someday we'll be there, too. We just gotta pray, and believe in God with all our hearts."

Her childlike trust nipped at his thoughts as he stared blindly at the words on the screen. Had he ever accepted his own faith with such absolute conviction? He'd been rebellious as a kid. Then he'd grown closer to his faith as an adult. Until…

The singing had stopped. The congregation was standing for prayer. He belatedly rose to his feet as the prayer ended and the pastor began to speak.

"Our first lesson for today is from Ephesians chapter 4. 'All bitterness, anger and wrath, insult and slander must be removed from you, along with all wickedness. And be kind and compassionate to one another, forgiving one another, just as God also forgave you in Christ.'

"Our second lesson is from Philippians chapter 4. 'Don't worry about anything; instead, pray about everything. Tell God what you need, and thank him for all He has done. If you do this, you will experience God's peace, which is far more wonderful than the human mind can understand. His peace will guard your hearts and minds as you live in Jesus Christ.' Please be seated."

Pastor Mark's rich baritone voice felt like a soothing balm as he moved on into his sermon, weaving those Bible verses into life's choices, mistakes and forgiveness. If he'd had a window into Logan's heart, he couldn't have chosen a message that hit home so perfectly.

Ah, forgiveness. It was easy to say, but so hard to do.

How did you forgive a surgeon who'd failed at a simple procedure to save his mom? The doctors who misdiagnosed his dad until it was too late? Cathy, with her calculated lies?

Or the God who had never listened to his prayers?

Each had caused immeasurable pain, a loss that could never be returned. Surely none of them had even given their responsibility for pain or suffering a second thought.

He felt his heart harden all over again. But this time, he took a slow, steadying breath and tried to let his anger go.

After church, Darcy asked Logan to stop by her house so she and Emma could change clothes and pick up her picnic basket.

On the drive out to his place, Emma chattered non-stop in the backseat of the pickup about puppies and horses, but Logan seemed unusually distant, and Darcy wondered if roping him into going to church had been a mistake. Had he felt out of place, still too new to the community to feel at ease in the company of so many close-knit strangers? Or had she said something wrong?

Now, after several hours of unpacking moving boxes

and putting things away, they all sat around his kitchen table, finishing off ham-and-cheese sandwiches, chips and quartered Honeycrisp apples,

When Emma wandered into the screened porch off the kitchen to play with her dolls, she set aside the last part of her sandwich. "You seem awfully quiet. Is something wrong?"

He took a last swallow of lemonade and didn't answer.

"I guess I was pretty thoughtless. I railroaded you into taking us to church, and didn't stop to think that maybe you're of a different faith and wouldn't want to attend ours. Is that it?"

"It's been a while since I've gone to church. You were right—he's a fine pastor, and he made me think. I'm glad I went."

But his solemn expression didn't change.

"Then what is it? Something's wrong."

"I didn't realize you'd lost your husband." He regarded her with troubled eyes. "Emma told me. I'm sorry, Darcy. I know it must have been really hard for you both."

She'd always accepted sympathies without offering any explanation, knowing the truth was so awkward, so revealing about her past life, that it tended to open an uncomfortable chasm in conversations that niceties couldn't bridge. And really, what could anyone say?

Dean had been unfaithful and she had been a fool.

But at the depth of compassion in Logan's voice, she knew she couldn't let any misconceptions lay between them.

She leaned back in her chair to look into the screened porch, where Emma was still occupied with her dolls but beyond hearing range. "It was…complicated," she said slowly, lowering her voice.

"You don't need to say anything. I know it's not my business."

"But it is, I guess. Whether we work in the same clinic or just in the same town, we might both have long careers here, and I don't want to hide the truth." She took a deep breath. "Dean and I were classmates in vet school. Love at first sight, married quickly. We had big plans. When we graduated, we went into a lot of debt developing a mixed equine and small-animal practice in a leased facility north of Minneapolis."

She ran a fingertip down the condensation on her glass of lemonade. "Dean had always wanted the best, and he made sure we bought it. But his taste for class didn't end with top-of-the-line ultrasound equipment and digital X-rays."

"I think I can guess what's coming."

She shrugged deflecting his sympathy. "Emma was just two when I discovered he was having an affair. He oversaw the office manager and the accounting while I spent my time away the clinic, being a mom. So I never noticed the billing discrepancies—money he'd diverted for entertaining his girlfriend, I guess. And I didn't realize that many of his late-night vet calls didn't actually involve horses."

"Ouch."

"Needless to say, when I found out, I felt like an absolute fool for trusting him. I guess it's not an un-common story—faithless husband, faithful wife—but it gets worse."

She glanced out at Emma once again to make sure

she was still in the screened porch and too far away to hear.

"A few months after he moved out, he was in the Caribbean with his gorgeous twentysomething girlfriend, living the high life on money he'd siphoned from our joint accounts before moving out. He had a scuba accident in deep water."

Logan's jaw dropped. "I'm so sorry. How in the world did you…"

"Of course, his latest girlfriend took off. At least she called to tell me about what happened, but she wanted no part of the funeral arrangements. I had friends who said I should just leave him down there—have his ashes scattered and be done with it. But what about Emma? It just didn't seem right. Would she need the closure of a service to remember and a grave to visit?" She sighed wearily. "After he left our practice, he had no life insurance. So a ton of paperwork and over fifteen grand later, he's now buried in Duluth, his hometown. And I'm still paying off those expenses, plus the loan I'd cosigned for his fancy new truck while we were still together."

"How did Emma take all of this?"

"She misses her dad terribly, though I hope she never hears the truth about him. But do I miss him? Not so much after all he did to destroy us and hurt his daughter. The verse from Ephesians at church today is actually what got me through it all, though I had to post it above the kitchen sink and recite it hundreds of times before the message finally got through. My anger was hurting only me. It had no effect on the one who caused it."

His eyes were deep with understanding, and she wondered what he might have been through in his own life.

"So," she added with a half smile, "you might be running into clients who think we'd be quite a pair, because they sure have said that to me. But I promise you I'm not ever going down that road again, so you don't need to worry. I've been there, done that, and it was a disaster—except that it gave me Emma. So never again."

"I bet there'll come a time…"

"Nope. *Never.*"

He laughed. "Then I guess that does make us quite a pair."

Curious now, she waited for him to elaborate, but he sat back in his chair and fell silent for a few moments before clearing his throat.

"I've been thinking about my original plans for the clinic. I agree with what you said earlier—that my original plans were narrow-minded. I was ignoring the obvious—that shutting down the small-animal clinic would be a big mistake."

"This is about misguided sympathy for me, isn't it?" she asked flatly. "But I can build a solo practice of my own. You should do what's best for you, not me."

"And that would be to keep the small-animal side going for the clients who already depend on it, with an associate vet who's excellent at what she does."

"You should think on this for a while. When you moved here, you—"

"I realize I was wrong."

She considered his words, then looked up and squarely met his gaze. "If we're truly talking business here, I want the chance to buy into the practice, just as I would've with Dr. Boyd—twenty percent per year, until I'm a full partner."

"Sounds fair enough."

"But if you decide otherwise, I'm going out on my

own. Let's take the next week to think this over, and then we can decide which way we want to go."

She'd kept an eye on Emma while they were talking, but now she wasn't in sight, and Darcy heard a faint telltale cough.

"Excuse me." She rose, grabbed her purse from the bench in the front entryway and hurried for the back porch.

Emma had curled into a ball on a wicker love seat, her dolls strewn across the floor. She coughed again when Darcy sat down next to her. "Hey sweetie, how are you doing? Want to sit in Mommy's lap?"

Darcy pulled her onto her lap to sit upright and stroked her back, then rested her fingertips lightly along Emma's ribs.

"Is she all right?" Logan pulled up a matching wicker chair and settled into it, watching them with an expression of concern.

"I think so. I don't hear her wheezing, and she's not laboring to breathe. But at the first cough I always start watching her closely, just in case." She kissed the top of Emma's head, then reached into her purse and withdrew a zippered vinyl bag. "We just want to be careful. Right, honey?"

Emma nodded somberly. "I get scared sometimes."

"I know you do, sweetheart, but we take really good care of you, right?" Darcy pulled a plastic peak-flow meter from the plastic bag, swiftly set it up and gave it to Emma. "Okay now…big breath out. Big breath in—and blow."

Emma dutifully blew into the plastic mouthpiece.

"Good job!" Darcy looked at the measurement showing along the length of the device, then had her do it once more. "Looks good, honey."

Logan asked, "So, it's okay?"

"Super. This gives us a measurement of lung function, and she's in her normal range. But I think she and I are just going to sit here for a while and have a nice rest. Then I'll get back to helping you out."

By late afternoon, the haphazardly placed furniture in Logan's great room and bedrooms had been arranged, and most of the paintings hung.

Now all of the moving boxes had been emptied and flattened as well, the kitchenware and linens stored.

Exhausted, Darcy took a final look around the main floor. "You have such a beautiful home. I love the woodwork and that massive stone fireplace."

"I barely glanced at the house when I flew in to look at the practice," Logan said with a rueful smile. "I'm just thankful it turned out to be a nice place and not a money pit."

"It's hardly that. And it's such a beautiful place for entertaining. Dr. Boyd used to host parties here for his staff and clients at Christmas and on the Fourth of July. No one ever wanted to miss his summer hog roast, or the gorgeous decorations at Christmas. He always had a dazzling twenty-foot tree in the great room, and the pine trees lining the driveway were covered in lights. Traditions to continue, right?" she teased.

"He must have had a team of elves to do all that," Logan said wryly as he adjusted a lampshade. "It must have taken weeks."

"He did it all himself for years, I understand. But by the time I came on board, he'd started hiring a decorating service for Christmas and a catering service for all of the parties." She glanced at her watch. "Well, I suppose we ought to go. Can you give us a lift?"

"Of course…unless you think Emma might like a ride. I saddled Drifter a few minutes ago, and she's ready to go."

Emma had been coloring at the kitchen table, but she whirled around at his words. "Really? I can ride a horse?"

"It's about time—you were a big helper today. You even colored some pictures for my fridge." He grinned down at her. "And I'm pretty sure I have just about every size of helmet in the tackroom, so we can find one your size."

They all walked in the shade of towering pines on the way out to the barn, the fallen needles under their feet releasing the crisp scent of pine.

Emma impulsively grabbed Logan's hand and skipped along beside him. "Someday I'm going to have a pony and ride all day long. At night, too."

Logan cast a glance over his shoulder at Darcy. "Hear that, Mom? You're going to need a larger yard *and* a barn. And you'll need a pony with headlights."

"That might be a while." Darcy leaned down to pick up a pine needle and crushed it between her fingers to release the Christmassy aroma. "But I look forward to it. I want her to have the same childhood I did."

He turned around and walked backward in front of her. "What kind of horses did you have?"

"A grade Welsh mare when I was six, which was a lot like giving me car keys. Then a gradual progression of horses after that, each one a little better. I lived on those horses. Mom said the only time she saw me in the house was when I was sick. I started showing horses when I turned eight, but when I started vet school, I no longer had time."

"Sounds like an idyllic childhood."

"It was, with incredible freedom. My friends and I rode bareback for miles in every direction on the roads and trails. I wouldn't let Emma do that now, though. The world is a scarier place. So, what about you?"

A corner of his mouth lifted in a faint grin. "You rode for fun. I was working cattle and helping start our two-year-olds under saddle. I think Dad thought my sister and I would break less easily if we got dumped, so he turned that job over to us when we got into middle school."

Later, as she stood along the fence and watched Logan patiently leading the palomino and her elated daughter up and down the long driveway for at least the twelfth time, her thoughts kept slipping back to the conversation after lunch.

She'd said what she'd truly believed, until now.

After Dean's cruel betrayal, she'd intended never to risk falling for anyone else. For whatever unknown reasons, Logan had said the same thing.

But those words had now carved an empty, aching place in her heart. Was that really what she wanted? To become lonely and bitter like her mom, and continue their long family legacy of failed relationships?

It didn't take any thought to imagine which would be the most positive example for Emma. But did Darcy have the courage to risk taking a chance?

Probably not.

She watched Logan sauntering toward her, his sleeves

rolled back, the first two buttons of his pale blue oxford shirt open to reveal his tanned throat. With those broad shoulders and his face shaded by his black cowboy hat and dark Oakley sunglasses, and he looked like a cowboy in a Levi's commercial.

The palomino's long white tail swept the ground as Logan turned her around and headed toward the highway once again. "Last trip," he called out over his shoulder. "Been a long day, and this cowboy's done for. But Emma thinks you should take a spin."

Delightful memories from her own youth deluged her as Darcy watched them return from their final trip up the lane and back.

The trail rides.

The horse shows.

And oh, the Minnesota State Fair—the most exciting of all. The cavernous cement arena had been called the Hippodrome back then, and every time she'd ridden through the wide entryway to compete in a quarter horse class, her adrenaline had soared and she hadn't been able to stop grinning.

After helping Emma dismount, she stepped lightly up into the saddle and adjusted her reins, the joy of being back on a horse again sending sparkles of delight down every nerve.

Logan looked up at her, his eyes twinkling. "I don't suppose we need to talk about the brakes."

"Probably not. But it's been a while."

He tipped his head in acknowledgment. "She was my reining horse, just so you know, and she did pretty well in working cow horse classes."

Power steering deluxe, then. Delight washed through

Darcy as she almost imperceptibly tensed the muscles of her calves and Drifter eased into a super slow jog on the soft grass-covered side of the lane, her head nice and low.

Darcy twisted in the saddle to look at Logan. "I may never bring her back. Is that okay?"

He laughed, but before he could answer, she cued the mare with a faint touch of a leg, and Drifter rocked into a slow lope, smooth as butter.

With other delicate cues, the mare did flying lead changes on the straightaway. Rollbacks and 360s, and when the highway came into view, Darcy sent her into a faster loop and cued her for a sliding stop.

Drifter sat down into the slide, as perfect as if she'd been headed for biggest shows in the country.

Awed, Darcy leaned forward to hug the horse's neck, then pivoted her toward the barn and let her saunter slowly on a loose rein during the half-mile trip home.

Back at the barn, Emma watched Darcy with amazement, and Logan leaned against the fence, one boot heel hooked on a fence board. The knowing look on his face made her grin in return.

"I haven't had a horse for years, and you just made my day. My week. Maybe my year," she breathed. "She's spectacular. I'd love to work cattle on her."

"Back in Montana, my sister and I showed quite a bit. The mare is definitely quick."

"I've never owned a reining or cutting horse, but I've ridden a few. It's so exhilarating—I can't even explain it. They make me feel like I'm dancing."

He looked up at her with a strange, indecipherable expression. "I know exactly what you mean."

She swung out of the saddle, tossed the stirrup over the seat, and rested a hand on the mare's neck. Drifter hadn't even broken a sweat. Her breathing was slow and steady.

Darcy paused with her hand on the girth. "Are you riding now, or do want me to unsaddle her?"

"Unsaddle. She's cool and doesn't need to be walked, but I can put her into one of the dry lots while I take you and Emma home."

"I don't suppose you'd like to sell her."

He chuckled. "Charlie and Drifter will never be sold."

"How about if I throw in my house? My car? Oh, wait. It doesn't run. Just the house, then. I don't have much else of value."

"Sorry. Not even your house." Laughing, he brushed an errant strand of hair away from her face. "But you and Emma are welcome to come out anytime."

"Tomorrow! Can we come tomorrow?" Emma begged. "Please?"

"Probably not, sweetie," Darcy said. "I'll be working all day, and you'll be at Mrs. Spencer's, playing with your friends. In the evening I need to work on your room. But maybe another time."

Emma didn't speak a word on the way home, and when they arrived she yawned and silently climbed down from Logan's truck.

"Looks like we're going to have a quiet evening," Darcy said as she followed Emma to the house with Logan at her side. "But I think she's just overtired. Thanks so much for the wonderful day."

At the steps of the porch Darcy impulsively gave Logan a quick hug and stepped back, suddenly feeling a little flustered and awkward at unexpectedly crossing that invisible line between friends and something more. Yet how could she regret something that felt so right?

Chapter Twelve

"Looks like the wrecker beat us here," Logan murmured when he took Darcy home on Monday after work. "Did they know where to take your car?"

"Red's. I talked to Red this morning, and he said he could at least check it over by tomorrow afternoon. He's going to drop off a loaner car after he gets done for the day. Just in case it doesn't come in time, Mrs. Spencer said she would drop Emma off after six."

"You've got one whole hour of freedom." He grinned at her. "So, what would you like to do?"

"I'll be prying up more pieces of that old linoleum in the kitchen. I figure at an hour every day, I'll be done in 2025. Easy."

"Perfect. Let's go in so I can help."

"Oh, no," she protested. "All of that prying and tugging can't be good for your shoulder. Anyway, I'm saving you for when the floors are all done so you can help me do the cabinets and countertops."

He followed her into the house anyhow, on the pretext of taking another look at the kitchen layout, but soon joined her on his hands and knees, shoving a scraper under the stubborn, brittle old flooring.

A wonderful aroma was emanating from a Crock-Pot on the counter, and he thought he detected the sweet scent of apple pie. If Darcy invited him to stay for supper, he definitely wouldn't be saying no.

"The bedrooms are both done, and the old wood flooring is beautiful," she said, blowing a lock of hair out of her eyes. "I thought of doing the living room next but decided to get the worst part over with. Isn't this fun?"

"Well worth the effort, though." He shoved his scraper under another piece of flooring that abruptly released and sent a small missile zinging across the room.

"It sure feels like it when you hit a spot where someone didn't go crazy with the glue." She sat back on her heels, grabbed a rubber band from the counter, and pulled her thick, wavy hair into a haphazard ponytail. "You can't imagine my elation when an entire two-foot-square section came off like a breeze. Best thing ever."

With what Darcy had already done on her own, they reached the middle of the room by the time Emma came home.

"That's it—I'm done," she announced. "Who wants supper?"

Just as he'd hoped, there was a beef roast in the Crock-Pot with tender whole potatoes, carrots and onions. The rich gravy surrounding it all was redolent with garlic and seasonings he couldn't name.

And after that came the pie. Wonderful pie.

The flaky, buttery crust sparkling with sugar crystals was perfection, the cinnamon-laced apples inside tender with just the right amount of juiciness.

"Thank you," he said when Darcy handed him a cup of coffee. He turned to Emma. "If I've ever had a better meal, I can't remember it. Your mom is an amazing cook."

Emma nodded. "I like macaroni better."

He hid a smile, remembering the neon-orange boxed macaroni of his childhood. "I'll bet that's good, too."

"We put lots of cheese in it, and crunchy stuff on the top."

"Those are buttery bread crumbs, Emma," Darcy said with a laugh. "Do you remember what else we use? You always help."

Emma's face scrunched into a frown. "Um...brown noodles."

"Whole wheat pasta."

"And...?"

"White stuff."

"A white sauce, with extra seasoning. Good job remembering, sweetie. Maybe you can help make it for Dr. Maxwell someday."

Not boxed macaroni and cheese. Homemade. He found himself wishing he could join them every day, instead of facing meat on the grill and a salad at his place, alone, week after week. "I would love that, Emma."

"Mommy would like that, too. And she *really* likes your horses." Emma nodded solemnly as she glanced between her mom and him, then brightened. "Maybe you could even be my daddy."

"Emma!" Darcy shot a mortified, warning look at her daughter, high color rising to her cheekbones.

The little matchmaker looked back at her, clearly mystified at why her mother was upset. "But you said—"

"I'm not sure what you think I said, but I have never

alluded to anything of the sort, and you just can't start asking guests something like that."

"What's *looded*?"

"*Alluded*. I didn't say..." Darcy made a small noise of frustration, but now her mouth was twitching as she tried to suppress a smile. "It's just that these things are between adults."

"Sienna has a daddy. And she gots a playhouse, too." Emma sat back in her chair, her lower lip thrust out in a pout, clearly thinking that Sienna had gotten a much better deal.

Ah, yes. The playhouse. Logan and his tomboy sister had grown up making forts up in the hayloft and ramshackle tree houses out in the cattle pastures with their cousins. But in a little girl's world in the Midwest, apparently playhouses were the ultimate prize.

Emma pushed her plate away. "Can I go now?"

"Yes, you may be excused." Darcy leaned out of her chair and caught her as she headed for the living room and gave her a hug. "Hannah says we can go back again tonight to see the puppies. Would you like that?"

"Yes!" All of her woes instantly forgotten, Emma threw her arms around her mother's neck and gave her a kiss on the cheek. "Now? Can we go now?"

"Dishes in the dishwasher first, and then we can go as soon as we get the loaner car."

Logan cleared the table while Darcy rinsed the dishes and put them in the dishwasher. "We should go together. I can drive, and I'd like to go out there anyway to check on Cedar."

"That poor, sweet dog. She probably has some ulcers under all of that matted fur."

He nodded. "Hannah was going to bring her in this

afternoon, but she had some sort of emergency at the hospital."

Emma pulled her shoes on at the speed of light and waited at the door. "I'm ready!"

All the way to Hannah's house she chattered nonstop, which precluded any other conversation.

"Sorry about that," Darcy said as they all got out of the truck.

"It's actually a revelation, discovering how much a four-year-old can talk."

The final wisps of sweet-smelling pine smoke drifted upward from the ashes in a metal fire ring in the backyard, scenting the air as they walked back to the barn behind Hannah's house.

Darcy shot an amused glance at him as they stepped inside the barn. "I remember rocking Emma as a baby, longing for the day when she could talk and tell me what she was thinking. Then she hit two, and hasn't stopped talking since."

Emma coughed as she made a beeline for Bonnie's cage. Darcy knelt beside her, quietly talking to her about caring for a dog.

Emma coughed again.

Logan went on to Cedar's pen and felt his heart grow heavy when he found the cage empty. The pile of soft blankets in the corner was missing, and even the feed and water bowls were gone.

Apparently Cedar hadn't made it.

"I should've taken her to the clinic when we were here last," he muttered, feeling a sense of loss. It had been three years since he'd lost his dog, and he'd never been able to bring himself to buy another.

He'd seen Cedar for only a short time, yet when her

soulful eyes had made that long connection with his, he'd simply known that he had to take her home.

Darcy looked up as he moved on to look at the other dogs, then the puppies. "Did you say something?"

"No…"

"It's been just a few days since we were here, but Bonnie already looks a little better, don't you think?"

The yellow lab was pressed against the front of her pen, wagging her tail, her attention focused on Emma. "Definitely a brighter affect."

"Hey, guys," Hannah called from the doorway. "Sorry I'm late. We roasted marshmallows after supper, and then I had to help with homework. I've got someone for Logan to see, but I can't bring her down here. Brace yourself. She looks far worse now."

He followed Hannah to the garage, where she kept an isolation pen.

His heart lifted when he saw Cedar curled up in a ball on fresh blankets. The heavy, tangled mats of hair had been clipped away, revealing ulcerations where the mats had pulled relentlessly at her skin. She had bald patches, as well.

"Besides everything else, the poor thing had the start of mange, as you can see," Hannah said unnecessarily. "I've seen it before, so when I started to clip her and discovered it, I took her up here to the isolation pen right away and disinfected everything she might have touched with bleach water. She had her first dip with a scabicide this evening, but from now on I'll do it weekly for a month."

"It's good you caught it." Logan looked down at the miserable dog, who had yet to lift her head at the sound of the voices nearby. "I'd like to bring her back to the clinic tonight to check this out under a microscope, if it's all right with you."

"Absolutely fine. Do whatever you need to do while she's there. I've got a kennel that you can borrow to put in the back of your truck."

"And…I'd rather not bring her back."

Hannah's eyes widened. "What?"

He smiled, remembering the depth of trust and intelligence in Cedar's golden-brown eyes when she'd finally responded to him the last time he'd been here. "Whatever the adoption fee is, I'll pay you right now. She's found her forever home with me."

Darcy scooped Emma into her arms and searched her pale face, then hurried through Hannah's yard. Once again she caught the scent of smoke, and again she felt a surge of trepidation when Emma broke into another spasm of coughing.

She stepped through the open back door of the garage and found Hannah and Logan deep in conversation on canine vaccinations.

She sank onto a folding chair with Emma in her lap. Now her coughing was tight. Wheezy. "I need my purse, now. Is the truck locked?"

"No." Logan glanced at them both. Then his eyes widened in alarm. He bolted out of the garage and returned in a moment with her purse. "Is everything in here?"

Hannah was a physician's assistant and had been down this road before. "Here, I'll find it."

She dug through the purse and found the clear plastic bag with Emma's asthma supplies, attached a clear plastic spacer to the quick-relief inhaler and placed it into Darcy's waiting palm.

Darcy shook it a couple times and depressed the top button. "Okay…big breath out…now a deeeep breath in—that's right. Hold it… Good. And another… Good girl."

Emma sagged against her, still pale, but in a few minutes the wheezing was lessening. Darcy rubbed her back in slow, comforting motions. "You'll be fine. Everything is fine."

Logan pulled up a folding chair next to her. "Hey, punkin, are you feeling better?"

Emma nodded almost imperceptibly, though Darcy knew how much even a light episode scared her. Who wouldn't panic if it was so hard to breathe?

"I'm so sorry—I wasn't even thinking when I let the kids have their little fire for marshmallows," Hannah said, her voice laced with regret. "I'll bet it was the wood smoke."

"Possibly." Darcy looked up at her. "But don't worry about it—she'll be fine."

Hannah rested a hand on Emma's shoulder. "Are her asthma episodes growing more frequent or worse?"

"No, though colds really exacerbate things, of course. The smoke sensitivity is fairly new."

"How often does she need the quick-relief inhaler?" Hannah asked.

"A few times a week at the most. Some weeks she's fine." Darcy dropped a kiss on Emma's head. "We haven't needed a trip to the ER in a long time. She's due to go into the clinic next month to see Dr. McClaren."

"You can get in sooner if need be," Hannah said. "Just give us a call."

* * *

It took only a few minutes for Logan to load Cedar into the plastic kennel and fasten it snugly in the back of the pickup, up against the cab so there'd be less of a breeze as he drove.

"What about Bonnie, Mommy? Can't we take her, too?" Emma twisted in her booster seat to look out the back window of the truck. "She could sit with me. *Please?*"

Darcy looked over her shoulder at Emma. "I told Hannah that we'll definitely take her, so don't worry. We're going to pick her up Sunday afternoon."

"Why not now?"

"Because I work the next four and a half days, and you'll be with Mrs. Spencer. We need to be home and spend time with her when she first comes to our house."

"You won't forget?"

"Of course not, sweetie."

"Promise?"

"Yes, of course. I promise."

"What about a pony?"

Logan laughed aloud and gave Darcy a sidelong glance that did something funny to her insides. "Yes, Mom. Why not a pony, too, as long as you're getting a dog?"

Darcy shot a dark look at him. "You are not helping."

The laugh lines at the corner of his eyes and the dimple in his right cheek deepened, but he kept his eyes on the road. After a few miles he glanced at the rearview mirror again. "Looks like your little cowgirl just fell asleep."

Darcy slumped in her seat. "That's not good. She'll wake up when we get home. A nap will set her bedtime back for a good hour—and that's if I'm lucky. She's quite a live wire at night."

"Maybe she can help you with the floor."

"You wait. Someday you'll have kids, and then you won't take these things lightly. Sleep means everything to a mom—or dad—who has to work every day."

"I suppose you're right," he said quietly, giving the rearview mirror another glance. "But I doubt I'll ever know firsthand."

When he pulled into her driveway, he parked behind an older model sedan with dents in the bumper and a Red's Auto frame around the license plate. He opened the back door of the truck. Emma was still asleep.

"I can get her," Darcy said, opening the opposite door.

"Nah, I've got her—you grab the booster seat." He lifted her into his arms and carried her to the front porch and waited while Darcy unlocked the door. Then he walked to Emma's bedroom and laid her on her twin bed.

"Looks like you just got a break," he whispered as he stepped back and watch Darcy carefully remove Emma's shoes and jeans and cover her with a light blanket. "Does she need her pajamas on?"

"That would be pushing my luck. She might even stay asleep for the night if I don't disturb her."

They both tiptoed out of the room, and Logan headed for the front door, where he hesitated, then turned back with a look of regret.

"I suppose I should get Cedar settled at the clinic."

She nodded, regretting the fact that he needed to leave. "I suppose."

"Thanks. For the wonderful meal. And for...the company."

"And thank you for helping with the floor, and taking us to Hannah's. And—" she considered her words "—thank you for being so sweet to Emma. I know it means a lot to her."

His gaze locked on hers. He took a single step closer, close enough that she could pick up his familiar scents of pine and fresh air, and a faint aftershave she couldn't name. And for just a moment she felt enchanted, as if she might be taking the most important step in her life.

But then he shook his head as if he'd felt that same connection and was just as afraid as she was. He walked out the door.

And the moment was lost.

Chapter Thirteen

With news spreading throughout the county about the new equine vet in Aspen Creek, Logan found his schedule filling up with farm calls. He spent most of his time on the road in his vet truck and very little at the clinic.

Foaling problems and other reproductive issues were always intense throughout the spring, often involving late-night calls, and there were a number of large horse breeding farms within a thirty-mile radius delighted to finally have a good equine vet in the area.

The hectic pace had helped him gain some perspective—along with a lot of time in his truck to think.

But now it was already Saturday afternoon, he'd spent the last hour in his office catching up on email and bills and reviewing Marilyn's accounting, and he needed to get to the airport in the Twin Cities on time or he'd hear about it for months.

"I'm off," he said to no one in particular. "See you folks Monday."

"You've got your cell phone, right?" Marilyn called out from the front office. "And you're on call this weekend?"

"Darcy is on for the rest of today. I've got Sunday."

"And you did talk to her, right? I left a couple messages on your desk."

He'd managed mostly to avoid Darcy since Monday night, when he'd been on the verge of sweeping her into his arms and kissing her senseless right there in her living room. What had come over him?

He'd thought a lot on the way home Monday night and during the four days since then. To his chagrin, he finally realized that she seemed to be avoiding him, as well, except for some brief businesslike exchanges.

"She knows she's on call tonight. I texted her."

"No, this is something else. It's about Emma, and an award, and a very important event. Something about the poor child facing a broken heart, if I understood correctly."

He glanced at his watch. "Darcy's already left for the day, and I've got to run. I'll call her later."

Marilyn's voice followed him down the hall as he waved to Kaycee and went out the back door. "Today. It has to be today."

Distracted by the news of a Middle East bombing on the public radio station, he was well into heavy traffic on southbound 494 before he remembered to call. Soon he was into even more traffic leading into the airport.

He had Susan in his truck and was headed out of the Twin Cities when his phone rang.

He grabbed his phone and pressed the screen to route the call from the hands-free speaker mode in the truck and into his cell. "Hello. This is Dr. Maxwell."

"So sorry to bother you," Darcy said, her voice tinged with embarrassment. "But I figured you hadn't gotten my message, and I promised Emma that I would try again. She's quite upset, thinking you won't be able to come."

He gripped the phone a little tighter. "What's this for?"

"Sunday school tomorrow, right after church. It's the last day of the classes until after Labor Day, and there'll be desserts and coffee, and prizes for the kids. She's getting an award for good attendance and is sure all of the kids will have both parents there, so she'll feel left out. She wonders if you could come as just her friend."

He glanced over at Susan. From her upraised eyebrow and knowing little smirk, he could tell she'd heard every word.

She shrugged. "Go for it. I don't mind. I'll probably sleep in anyway."

He returned to the call. "What time?"

There was a long pause. "I'm so sorry—I forgot you were having company. I didn't mean to interrupt."

She hung up before he could say another word.

"Sounds like she's not too happy." Susan rolled her eyes. "Tell me she's not another girlfriend like that last doozy. Puh-leeze."

"The woman on the phone is the other vet at the clinic."

"All the better, bro. Mutual interests and all that?"

He ignored her little jibe and focused on the slow-down of the traffic ahead. "So, how are the kids? I haven't seen them since Christmas."

"They're with their dad for the weekend, probably driving him crazy. I figure it serves him right." She looked away. "I just needed some time to get away and think things through, you know? Big decision."

Logan spared her a quick glance. "How did the counseling go?"

She snorted. "Would've helped if Rick had decided to go. But he never would've admitted to any responsibility for our problems, anyhow."

"Did it help you to talk to someone?"

"I went a few times, then gave up. One side of the story couldn't ever get to the real problems, right?" She bit her lower lip. For all her bravado, Logan saw a single tear trail down her cheek.

"I'm so sorry, sis."

"Me, too." She laced her fingers on her lap. "You know, if he had just made a little effort—tried to help around the place, or offered to help with the kids' homework once in a while—I would have been okay with that. But he was gone most of the time and impatient when he got home. The house was never clean enough. He didn't like what I made for dinner. Where was his underwear, and why didn't I have the lawn mowed before he got home? Enough is enough."

Enough is enough was probably Rick's assessment, as well. As for her part in this mess, Logan knew that Susan had perpetually run up heavy debts by shopping at high-end stores and never seemed satisfied with what she had. But he'd wisely learned to hold his tongue on that score.

One wrong word and she would rail that he was always on her husband's side and neither of them had ever loved her, and then there would be no chance at all to get through to her.

"If it's all that bad, then I'd say you deserve better. Want me to go back to Montana and give him what-for?"

She gave him a watery smile. "He would back down if he saw you coming, but I doubt it would make any difference in the long run."

"So, how long are you staying here?"

"Just 'til Monday afternoon. Much as I'd like to stay away longer, Rick has an important company meeting in Houston, so I have to get back to take care of the kids."

He reached across the cab to give her hand a quick squeeze. "I'm glad you came."

"It's funny, the things you imagine when you're young…" Her voice turned wistful. "A knight in shining armor sweeping you away. Buckets of money. A loving family. Growing old together, and still in love after fifty years. Then reality comes along to remind you that life just doesn't end up that way, except in the movies. Of course you know all that—you were going to marry that despicable woman in Montana, and then she tried to drag you down with her. What did she get? Was it twenty years?

"Something like that." He sighed heavily. "She had everyone at the clinic fooled. Most of all me."

"Which just proves my point." Susan wearily leaned against the headrest and rolled her head to face him. "Mom and Dad divorced, then Uncle Jake, and two of my best friends did, too. I've come to realize that it's a mistake to think you're going to be happy, because eventually everything just turns to dust. You're the only one in our family who's smart enough to stay single."

After they made it to Aspen Creek, he looked in on Cedar at the clinic, then drove home and got Susan settled in an upstairs guest room.

Down in the great room, he turned off the lights and settled in his favorite leather chair to stare at the moonlit landscape outside. With the windows open, he could hear the wind sighing through the trees and inhale the sweet scent of pine that was so reminiscent of his life back in Montana.

One of the horses whinnied, and in the distance coyotes were yip-yipping to the moon. All he needed was the sound of a few beef cattle bawling now and then to feel right at home, but in a year or so he would have a herd established here. With a return to cattle ranching and his vet practice, his life would be complete.

But though Montana had been his home, he had no yearning to go back. It held only bitter memories now.

The only one smart enough to stay single.

His sister's words rolled through his thoughts again and again, a litany that might have been meant as praise but only reminded him of how empty his life had become.

Darcy was struggling financially under the burden of her profligate husband's thoughtlessness. She didn't have a fancy house or a fine car. She was the sole support of her little family with all of the heavy responsibilities that went with it.

But she had what really mattered, and it reminded him of what he had lost.

A cozy and welcoming home. A sweet child or two. A life of someone to talk with over dinner and bedtime stories to read at night.

These were the things he'd longed to have, when he thought he was going to marry Cathy. The opportunities he'd lost when she betrayed him.

But his life was going to get better. He might be totally gun-shy when it came to risking his heart ever again. But in a few days he could bring Cedar home from the clinic, and at least he'd have a dog.

In the morning, he'd heard no footsteps moving around upstairs and Susan hadn't started a pot of coffee in the kitchen, so Logan assumed she was still sleeping. He drove to church with just minutes to spare.

The congregation was seated and already singing a beautiful old hymn when he slid into the back pew. He looked around, seeing things he hadn't noticed the last time when he felt awkward and out of place.

Beautiful old stained-glass windows—six on each side. The sunlight beaming in from the east that splashed the parishioners with jewel-like colors.

He knew the building was very old—a plaque on the outside proclaimed it was on the Register of Historic Places. But the soft ivory paint looked freshly done, the woodwork gleamed with loving care and the windows sparkled.

Throughout the service, the Bible verses Pastor Mark used and the sermon he gave flowed over him. The heartfelt praise songs seemed to lift him up. During the final prayer, he looked up at the brass cross hanging over the altar and realized that this place filled him with an utter sense of peace. Forgiveness. And even an unexpected ray of hope that seemed to fill in some of the ragged and empty places in his heart.

And he found that for the first time in his sorry life, he wished a church service wasn't already over.

Afterward he couldn't see Darcy and Emma anywhere in the crowd drifting down the central aisle to shake the pastor's hand, so he stayed at the back until the line thinned out, then joined the stragglers.

Someone slid a hand around his elbow. "Howdy, stranger," she chirped. "So good to see you here."

It was Hannah.

"Glad to be here."

"That tall guy over there—talking to the lawyer—is my fiancé, Ethan. I'll make sure he comes over and says hello if Walter ever stops talking."

"Actually, I'm looking for Emma and Darcy. They're at some sort of Sunday school ceremony."

"Downstairs. The kids and parents were mostly sitting in the back during the service and slipped away during the last song so they could get ready." She pointed to the right. "The stairway is over there."

He nodded his thanks and descended to the lower level, where apparently everyone in Aspen Creek had gathered. Chairs and tables with tablecloths had been placed around the large meeting hall, but there were so many people standing that he had no idea where to look for Emma.

Beth appeared at his side. "You did come! Emma will be so happy." She pointed to the opposite side of the room. "You should find her over there with her mom. The little ceremony will be starting soon, but don't worry—it shouldn't take more than an hour."

Logan made his way sideways through the crowd, apologizing as he went. When he finally spied Emma, he smiled at her. "Hi, little lady. I hear you've having a big day."

She squealed with delight and rushed to him, her flouncy pink skirt bouncing and her arms raised, so he scooped her up into his arms.

She wasn't his, yet he felt such a surge of protectiveness just holding her that it nearly took his breath away.

"I knew you'd come! Mommy didn't think so, but I *knew* you would."

Darcy materialized in front of him with a small cup of pink punch. "You don't want to spill your punch on Dr. Maxwell, so you'd better hop down, honey."

Emma wrapped her arms wrapped her arms around his neck. "No."

"Let me set your drink aside, then." She looked up at Logan with a grateful smile. "I just figured that you had company and wouldn't want to come. Thank you so much. As you can see, it means a lot to Emma."

"I'm glad you let me know. Susan is still asleep back home or I would've brought her."

Darcy's welcoming expression shuttered. "That would have been very…nice. I hope you two have a great time."

"It won't be, but I'm glad she came. She's pondering the end of her marriage and just wanted to get away."

"Oh." Darcy blinked. "Oh, dear. I'm sorry."

"It's not the first time, unfortunately. But she's my only sister, and I always do whatever I can to help."

Ever since she'd heard Logan mention he was having company this weekend, Darcy had envisioned him with a beautiful girlfriend from back in Montana. Probably a mad, passionate affair with marriage on the horizon.

She'd found herself feeling a deep sense of loss over what could never be.

Which made no sense at all.

After her experience with Dean, she'd been so sure that she'd never fall for anyone again, for nothing could be worth risking such crushing heartache.

Yet despite her convictions, and her doubts about him when they first met, Logan had proved to be the kind of guy she'd once dreamed of meeting, and she'd found herself falling for him a little more with every passing week. And more than that, he was wonderful with Emma, who idolized him. He'd once said he would never have kids, but how could that be?

Discovering that Logan's weekend guest was his sister had literally taken Darcy's breath away. But still...

A loudspeaker squawked.

At the far end of the meeting hall, the head of the Sunday school program gripped a microphone and began reading off the names of the children who had won prizes for memorization. Then she began reading the perfect attendance list from youngest on up.

Darcy looked up at Emma, who still refused to leave Logan's arms. "You need to get down, sweetie. She's about to call your name."

Logan swung Emma down to the floor and watched as she fell into line with the other four-year-olds. As the little ones marched across the stage, Emma waved at Darcy and Logan, her face beaming with pride.

Someone touched Darcy's arm, and she turned to see one of the older women in the church whose name she couldn't recall.

"You have such a lovely family," the woman said in a loud whisper. "You must be so proud. Such a handsome young husband and pretty little daughter. Not many families stay together these days."

Her voice was one that carried.

Embarrassed, Darcy smiled at her and edged away. She caught a glimpse of Beth giving her a sympathetic smile through the crowd.

She didn't even want to imagine what Logan thought of the elderly woman's assumption after he'd been so kind to show up. He'd made it clear that he had no intention of ever settling down.

"Let's go," she whispered to him, as soon as Emma came back to her side. "This program will take a while."

It took time to make it through the crowded room, but once they made it outside, she took a deep breath of fresh air.

Emma lifted her certificate up high. "I got good 'tendance. And I learned a *lot*."

"I'll bet you did, Emma," Logan said. "Great job."

"Did you get good 'tendance, too?"

"Yes, ma'am. My mom and dad made sure of it. And I'm still learning."

Emma spied some dandelions scattered like little disks of sunshine in the grass and bent to pick them.

Darcy waited until she was completely engrossed, then touched Logan's sleeve. "Thank you again for coming. It meant all the world to her."

"Glad to do it. It got me back to church again, and I'm beginning to realize just how much I've missed it."

"You were there? You could have joined us—" She bit her lip, realizing that he might have intentionally found a different pew.

"I didn't see you or I would have. I got there a little late."

"I-I'm really sorry if you were embarrassed about what the woman said downstairs. I didn't know what to say without making a scene."

"Any man in that room would be honored to claim you and Emma as his family." He went very still, his expression unfathomable as he searched her face. "You said you were never taking a chance again, but no one with a decent heart would ever treat you like your husband did. I can promise you that."

She watched him head for his pickup, feeling a little breathless and more than a little confused. Had he just encouraged her to look elsewhere, or had he meant those words for himself?

Chapter Fourteen

After getting home from church and making lunch, Darcy called Hannah to arrange a time for picking up Emma's new dog, but as Hannah and Ethan were leaving to check out wedding venues, they promised to drop Bonnie off on their way.

Emma was overcome with awe when Hannah appeared at the front door with Bonnie at her side.

"She's here! She's really here!" Too excited to contain herself, she ran in circles and jumped up and down, her arms flailing, then threw her arms around Darcy's legs.

Clearly terrified, Bonnie yelped and scrambled backward.

"This probably isn't the best introduction," Hannah said dryly as she reached down to comfort the dog. "Got any suggestions?"

"Emma and I need to have a little talk." Darcy said with an apologetic smile. "Can we meet you in the backyard in a couple minutes?"

Darcy closed the front door, then knelt down and rested her hands on Emma's shoulders. "Have you ever been really scared about something? So scared you just wanted to run and hide?"

Emma nodded.

"Well, poor Bonnie is really scared, too. She had a good home, then ended up at Hannah's rescue center where there were strange people and noisy dogs that frightened her, because she only knew her quiet home with an elderly man. And now she's here, facing another change."

Emma's eyes filled with worry. "She doesn't want to come here?"

"She'll be fun and playful later, but right now we want to make it easy for her to get to know us. So you need to be slow and quiet and very gentle. Can you do that?"

Emma nodded and took Darcy's hand.

"Let's go, then. Just don't forget. Today is a quiet day."

Hannah was in the backyard with Bonnie still on the leash when they came outside.

The golden lab tentatively wagged its tail when Darcy and Emma approached.

"Let's sit down on the picnic bench, sweetie, and let her come up to you. But don't grab her around the neck—at least for now. Dogs can see that as a form of aggression."

Emma sat quietly as the dog nervously surveyed her surroundings, then slowly approached and sniffed her knee. "I hope you like us, Bonnie. You're going to be my friend."

The lab sat down and rested her head on Emma's lap.

"Looks good to me," Hannah said. "Now I'd better

get going, because Ethan has the car running. Let me know if you have any problems."

After Hannah shut the gate behind her, Darcy stood and unsnapped the leash. "Let's let her explore her new home, all right?"

Emma giggled as the dog crisscrossed the yard at a jog, nose to the ground. She explored every nook and cranny. Sized up the fence. When a squirrel chattered from its perch on an overhead branch, Bonnie launched into a volley of barks. Then she stared at the screened porch and tentatively rested a paw on the lowest step. Every few minutes, she came back to Emma and nudged her knee with her nose as if asking her to join her.

"I'd say this went just fine," Darcy said with a smile. "Let's let her check out the house."

Inside, the dog continued checking every corner, until at last she settled down and followed Emma into her room. She curled up on the rug by the bed, watching Emma play with her dolls.

"If everything's all right, I'm going to go back to the kitchen and figure out what we're having for supper. Call if you need me, okay?"

Darcy hunted through the freezer and pulled out a package of chicken thighs that she defrosted in the microwave, then threw into the Crock-Pot on high with seasonings, sliced onions and barbecue sauce.

Eyeing the floor, she dropped to her knees and chipped at another section of the vinyl. She sat back on her heels with awe when a large section came up. *Thank You, Lord.*

The next piece came up just as easily, and soon she had the final section pulled free and the hardwood floor exposed. Overjoyed, she called out to Emma to come see what she'd accomplished.

Emma didn't answer.

Frowning, Darcy jumped to her feet and hurried back to the bedrooms. "Emma?"

Success.

She was lying on her bed, a book in her hands, with her head on Bonnie's side. And both were fast asleep.

When her cell phone rang twenty minutes later, Darcy had finished hauling out the last of the vinyl and was busy scraping at the pools of petrified flooring glue that remained.

Surprised at the Montana number on the screen, she set aside her scraper and answered the call.

"Hey, this is Susan—Logan's sister. I made him give me your number."

Baffled, Darcy tried to image any reason why she would call. "Is he all right?"

Susan laughed. "More than. I insisted that I wanted you and your daughter to join us for supper, but he thought you'd be busy—something about a floor. I told him that was a lame excuse to not ask. We'll eat at six, if that works for you?"

This wasn't just an invitation, it was an expectation. "I—I guess so."

"Don't worry—this isn't the Inquisition or anything. I'm just curious about what he's gotten himself into by moving so far away, and figured it would be nice to meet you. He says you're going to be his business partner."

Talking to her was like an encounter with a steamroller, and Darcy felt a little breathless. "He did? We've discussed it, but nothing is final yet."

"Whatever. Six, then?"

"That's good. What can I bring?"

Susan bellowed at her brother, her voice muffled. Then she came back to the call. "He says some sort of easy dessert would be good. Maybe brownies? But you really don't have to bother. He's got ice cream here."

Darcy turned the Crock-Pot to low so the chicken would be done around bedtime and could be refrigerated for dinner tomorrow. Then she considered her ravaged kitchen before reaching for one of the three-ring binders where she kept her favorite recipes protected in plastic sleeves.

Something easy, yes. But she had no doubt about Susan's intent. Tonight she would be assessed and probably found wanting as part of Logan's new practice. Darcy had a feeling that people did not pass muster with his sister, no matter who they were.

But she wasn't going to fail at dessert.

At six, Darcy pulled up at Logan's place and helped Emma out of the car, then reached for the handle of her covered pie carrier.

"I think Bonnie will be lonely at home," Emma said with a worried frown. "Should we go get her?"

"She's better off at home—especially on her first day with us. She'll be fine in the house."

As they walked up to Logan's front door, Darcy started imagining what they would find. From Susan's strong voice and no-nonsense attitude, she expected a woman topping six feet with broad shoulders, just like her brother. Someone who was a serious contender in women's boxing.

When the door opened, Darcy felt her jaw drop.

Susan offered a delicate hand. "You must be Darcy. I'm so glad to meet you—and this young lady must be Emma."

Susan was all of five feet tall, probably a hundred pounds, with bright blue eyes and a tumble of blond curls down her back. If she wasn't doing some sort of petite modeling or television work, she was seriously missing a golden opportunity.

Darcy blinked. "So nice to meet you."

"Logan just put the steaks on, and we've got romaine salad, garlic French bread and baked potatoes. That seems to be his only skill set, so I hope it's all right. Won't you come in?"

She led the way out to the screened porch in back, where the table was set and a bright profusion of wild-flowers had been arranged in a quart-size canning jar.

Logan was at the grill on the stone patio beyond. Setting aside his long barbecue fork, he came inside. "So you've met, I suppose? Susan, Emma just won a big award at Sunday school today."

"You were in church?" Susan eyed him closely, her eyes sharp and assessing. Then she smiled and offered her hand to Emma. "Congratulations. Your mom must be very proud."

Emma nodded, her gaze veering toward a low set of shelves where Logan kept a stack of paper and a box of crayons. "Can I color now?"

"Of course." Susan watched her collect the supplies and spread them on a glass-topped wicker coffee table in front of a matching wicker love seat. "I can see that you know where things are around here. Help yourself."

Susan and Darcy brought out the foil-wrapped potatoes, salads and dressing. By then, Logan was bringing the foil-wrapped French bread redolent with garlic and butter and a platter of juicy rib eyes.

If steaks were Logan's one achievement in the culinary arts, at least he was a star.

When everyone was seated, Susan gave Logan a pointed look. "Grace?"

He nodded.

They all reached for a neighboring hand and said a simple table prayer. Then Logan passed the steaks. "The most rare are on the right."

Darcy cut part of her steak and put tiny pieces on Emma's plate, along with a buttered half of her baked potato and some diced lettuce.

She then cut a bite of steak for herself. "Oh, my. This steak is perfection."

"It's the maître d'hôtel butter." Susan looked up at her. "He adds it on top at the very last minute, then it melts over the grilled meat. Butter, a little fresh parsley, lemon, garlic, salt and pepper. Our mom always used it, too. And growing up on a cattle ranch, we learned to use only prime beef when it comes to steak."

Darcy looked over at Logan and smiled. "I am in awe. Everything is just wonderful."

While they were finishing the meal, Susan and Logan intelligently debated politics and world news, then segued into the Colorado Rockies game stats and whether they had a good chance this year.

Whatever his opinion, Susan automatically took the opposite view. The competitive conversation was like watching a tennis match that had been choreographed to a fine point over the years.

Content just to listen, Darcy smiled, intrigued by this side of him.

Susan broke off the debate with her brother and looked at Emma. "I hear you love horses. I'll bet Logan would saddle up a horse if you'd like to ride. Then we could enjoy dessert afterward."

Emma nodded vigorously, but Darcy shook her head. "Really, we can't take more of your time. I'm sure you'd much rather visit with each other. And honestly, we really can't stay that long. We got a new dog today, and she's in the house."

"Kenneled, right?"

"Um…yes, but…"

Susan shrugged. "It won't take Logan long to bring a horse up from the barn. It looks like Emma is more than a little excited."

Of course she was. After that enticing invitation, she was bouncing in her chair.

From the look Logan gave his sister as he stood, he suspected that she'd just skillfully engineered a setup.

"Behave," he said quietly to her as he headed for the screen door.

"Can I come with you now? Please?" Emma quivered with anticipation. "I won't be in the way."

He extended a hand. She scrambled out of her chair and held on to it as they headed through the backyard toward the barn.

Darcy rose and began gathering plates, while Susan picked up the serving dishes. "Thanks again. This was all lovely, but I do hope we didn't intrude on your time together. You leave tomorrow, right?"

"Back to the soap opera that is my life." Susan raised an eyebrow. "I assume Logan told you about why I'm here."

"Um…"

"No worries. I assumed he did." She gave a rueful laugh as she began loading the dishwasher. "I seem to be an expert at finding good men. I'm just not so good at keeping them. So, how about you? Were you married long?"

"What?"

"You have to admit that any good sister would worry about her little brother, especially after what he's been through. I worry about him making another mistake."

"Unless you're talking about a business relationship, I think there's been a misunderstanding. He and I aren't…an item."

Susan stopped, a dirty plate in hand, and turned to give her a flat look of disbelief. "Really."

"I work at the clinic. I may well buy into the practice and become a partner. And I think we're becoming friends. Nothing more." She shrugged. "Anyway, just in passing conversation, he has mentioned that he has no plans to settle down with anyone. Not ever. So take it up with him, but it doesn't sound like you have any reason for concern."

"And yet he's gone to church with you. Twice."

Darcy gave a helpless little shrug. "As coworkers. Friends. It's not uncommon."

"For him it is. Logan has not stepped into a church since our mom and dad died. He's been angry about what happened to them for so long that I thought it would never happen. And yet he apparently put those feel-

ings aside. For you. And after that deal with Cathy—"
She broke off and studied Darcy's face closely. "So you
don't know?"

"Know what?"

Susan seemed to reconsider her words. "I thought he
would never take a chance on someone new, yet here
he is. Why?"

"I—I have no idea." But from somewhere deep in
her memory, Kaycee's narrowed look at Logan and her
words *glass houses* and *throwing stones* surfaced.

Maybe it was time to do some sleuthing on her own,
because neither Kaycee nor Susan was very forthcom-
ing.

"Understand that I have nothing against you. You
seem like a great person." Susan dropped the plate in
the dishwasher and shut the door. Her voice gentled, but
it also held a thread of steel. "But I didn't come here to
think over my marriage—I already know which way
that's going. I came here because of you."

Shocked, Darcy stared at her. "Me?"

"Logan and I talk on the phone almost every week,
and I could tell something was different. After a lot of
badgering, I finally got just a little information out of
him. How he's spending time with you outside work.
How much he likes your daughter."

"But really, there's nothing going on here. He helps
out with some things at my house because of an auction."

"I think there's more—at least, on his part."

Darcy felt a warm little ember come to life in her
heart, even though she knew what Susan said wasn't
true.

"Apparently there's a lot you don't know about his

past, but you won't find anyone on this planet better than my brother. But I promise you—I won't let you break his heart. Because if you do, you'll be answering to me."

Chapter Fifteen

On Monday, Logan took Susan back to the airport—a strangely silent trip. Then he returned to Aspen Creek and discovered two emergency calls added to his already full schedule.

The rest of the week sped by—equally hectic, despite the fact that few mares were still foaling in late May, and the breeding season for next year was essentially over.

He'd barely seen Darcy since dinner last Sunday afternoon beyond some passing, casual greetings at the clinic. But today he was done and back at the clinic by five, determined to catch her before she went home. He'd spent the week feeling edgy and out of sorts, like he'd lost something but didn't know how to get it back.

And he suspected Susan had something to do with it.

He waited until Kaycee and Marilyn left for home at five thirty, then found Darcy in the lab running a CBC in the hematology analyzer. "Is this for someone in an exam room?"

She shook her head. "A dog we're keeping overnight. What's up?"

"I couldn't get a thing out of my sister before she left, but I get the feeling that she might have been—" he searched for the right word, but when it came to Susan, that could be a challenge "—intrusive."

Darcy's shoulders sagged as she turned to face him. "I honestly had no idea what she was talking about, but she seemed to think an awful lot of hanky-panky was going on around here. Apparently—don't laugh— between you and me."

"I figured as much."

"She also hinted at all sorts of big secrets in your past. And—" Darcy gave a helpless laugh "—I actually think she threatened me, sort of. Not that I took her seriously. I mean, she's got to be under five feet tall."

"That's where a lot of people underestimate her," he said with a wry smile. "She wrestled me to the ground and broke my arm when she was only ten."

"Maybe so. But as an adult, she seems like a wonderful sister who just wants to watch out for her brother, and I respect that."

He sighed, remembering some of the times when she'd tried to interfere a bit too much. "I'd like to discuss this a little more, but not here. Could you meet me for dinner tonight—just you and me?"

Her gaze flickered. Then she turned back to the analyzer. "I've got Emma, remember?"

"Could you find a sitter for an hour or two? There's a little restaurant out by the lake. Excellent food, and it's quiet."

"I just don't have anyone I can call on such short notice."

"At least let me stop at your house so we can measure the cabinets. Then you can get them ordered whenever you're ready."

"The sooner the better." She glanced up at the clock. "I'll have just forty-five minutes before I need to pick her up, so we'll have to make this quick."

After closing up the clinic and setting the alarm, Logan followed Darcy to her house and parked in front. From inside came the sound of loud barking until Darcy unlocked the door and called out Bonnie's name.

"I'm glad to have an alarm system again," she said with a smile as she let the dog out into the backyard. "She sounds so fierce, no one would ever guess she's such a softy."

"So it's worked out well?"

"More than. She's housebroken, she doesn't chew on things and she's totally devoted to Emma—follows her around like a shadow and sleeps on the foot of her bed." Darcy filled a stainless-steel dog bowl with kibble and set it back down on the floor. "I always recommend that clients check the local shelters for an older dog before bringing home a puppy, and this is why. How's Cedar?"

"A little better," he admitted. "I brought her home a week ago. She's had three dips in scabicide, so the mange is clearing up and her bald spots have peach fuzz coming in. I keep telling her she's quite the fashion plate, but I don't think she believes me."

Darcy laughed. "Just don't let her look in any mirrors."

"The housebreaking is going fairly well. I don't think she'd ever been inside before, so that scared her. And she hadn't ever learned all of the good citizenship rules. But it's coming along. Once her coat has grown back,

I'll start taking her to the clinic and on calls with me so she's not alone all day."

"A perfect life, then, if she can be with you 24/7." She looked at her wristwatch. "So, what did you want to discuss? I'll need to go after Emma before long."

He blew out a long sigh. "As I started to say at the clinic, I want to apologize for my sister. When she got Emma excited about riding Drifter last Sunday and sent the two of us off to the barn, I figured she had a reason. I thought she might pry a little, but not that she'd go so far."

"She's worried about you."

"But it wasn't appropriate for her to interfere, or to try to warn you away."

"It was lovely to see someone who cares so much for family that they'll try to intercede. But as much as I do like her, it wasn't really necessary." Darcy gave a dismissive wave of her hand. "You'd already made it clear that you aren't looking for any relationships here in town. It sounded to me like you were saying 'been there, done that, not going through it again.' And as you might imagine, I can totally empathize. So, case closed."

"I need to talk to you about something else that I should have told you already, but it's a little complicated, and we don't have enough time." His gaze fell on a stapled, typed list several pages long that she'd left on the counter. "Veterinary equipment?"

A blush rose to her cheekbones. "With costs, for either a storefront office or a mobile vet clinic. It makes me a little dizzy to look at those numbers, but I want to be prepared either way."

"You talked about buying into the practice. Staying on board," he said slowly. "Is that off the table now?"

"Of course not. But we haven't really sat down to talk it over yet, either. Without any concrete numbers, I don't know which direction is the best way for me to go. So I just want to keep my options open."

He nodded. "I need to talk to the bank and also my lawyer. When I get something drawn up for you to consider, I'll let you know."

"Perfect. So, what do you think of the kitchen floor?"

He surveyed the bare hardwood, impressed. It still needed all the steps of finishing, but the vinyl was gone, and a thorough sanding made it look a hundred times better. "You did all this?"

"Worked on it every night. The bedroom floors are completely done. Last night I ran the barrel sander and edger over the kitchen floor, so next I can apply the sealer." She reached for a tape measure on the kitchen counter. "Once we take the measurements, I can do some ordering."

"What have you decided?"

"At first I wanted to just reface the cabinets. But after studying the poor condition of these, I'd rather replace them all. White upper and lower, with granite counters—ideally white with gray veining."

"Sounds good."

"I've chosen the style of cupboards in a catalog at the lumberyard. The lower ones have soft-close drawers, and some have special dividers. There are even toe kick drawers at the very bottom, floor level, to add more storage."

He looked at her in awe. "You amaze me."

"The floors have taken hours of unskilled labor and

a lot of YouTube videos while trying to get it right. The cabinets I just need to choose."

"I mean everything. Your skill as a vet and dedication as a mom. Doing all of this work on the house yourself would overwhelm a lot of people. And then there's your cooking. That dessert you brought Sunday night was amazing. Cloud—"

"No, *kladdkaka*." She grinned, her hazel eyes sparkling. "Pays to know a Scandinavian, I guess. We have the best desserts. And that one took just ten minutes in the oven."

"I've never had anything like it. It tasted like chocolate silk."

"Well, now. You might need to stop by now and then for supper, just to see what we're having."

They got down to work taking measurements, then checked them a second time.

By then it was time to go. They both headed out the front door onto the porch, and she locked the door behind them. "I really appreciate your help with this. I'll order the cabinets tomorrow and let you know when they're ready."

He gave her a quick one-arm hug, then caught her hand in his and gave it a little squeeze. "I just hope you'll like it all when you're done."

The shadows under the covered porch and the lowering sun made the space seem more intimate somehow, more private. When he drew her a little closer, she didn't resist.

And then, without a plan or even conscious thought, he bent down and kissed her.

Chapter Sixteen

Startled, Darcy stiffened, then found herself melting into Logan's kiss. A sparkling sensation washed through her, filling her with warmth and wonder.

Despite every resolution she'd made since Dean walked out on her, she curved her arms around Logan's neck, pulling him even closer.

It was Logan who finally broke away.

He smiled down at her with that little half smile that deepened just one of his dimples, sending a shiver of awareness down her spine. His eyes darkened as their eyes locked.

Then he dropped another swift, gentle kiss on her mouth that sent Fourth of July sparklers coursing through her veins all over again. And in that brief, sweet moment, he left her longing for more.

When had she ever felt that way? Dazed, she tried to collect her thoughts as he jogged out to his truck.

The answer was *never*.

Not with Dean. Certainly not with anyone else she'd ever dated.

She stood on the porch well after Logan's taillights disappeared down the street.

True, it had been so long since she'd been in Dean's arms that she could barely remember any emotion he might have stirred, and now even those fading memories were clouded by his deceptions.

Had he ever really cared for her? Loved her? Had there ever been a time when their relationship had been honest and real?

She'd thought so…but maybe she'd only been a convenience. Easy prey. Just a bright student at the top of their class who would thus be a good money earner. A logical choice. Another set of hands at the clinic.

Maybe he'd been having affairs all along and she'd been too blind to notice, caught up as she was with caring for their daughter, and working day and night to make their new clinic succeed.

But that was the past and this was now. And this felt different.

Even now she imagined she could still detect Logan's crisp aftershave and the fresh scent of soap on his skin.

Shaking off her thoughts, she hurried to Mrs. Spencer's to pick up Emma with just minutes to spare.

"You look funny, Mommy," Emma announced when Darcy walked in. "You're pink."

"Hmm…must've been the nice spring sun today."

Mrs. Spencer, a hefty woman shaped like a barrel, was no-nonsense and plainspoken with adults, but she enthralled kids from infancy to teens with her sense of humor and a laugh that shook her belly.

Now she gave Darcy a head-to-toe perusal and pursed her lips. "I'd say it might be that handsome young vet of yours. He could make a statue blush."

"Mrs. Spencer." Darcy glanced around the living room, hoping there were no other adults around. "Please."

The older woman's ample middle shook as she chuckled. "From the chatter down at the cafe, I'd say everyone in town knows there's something going on between you two. Don't think it's any secret."

"Well, tell everyone in town that it isn't true. We've not gone on so much as a single date. I just work for him. And…I won him at that church auction, so that's why he's been doing some work at my house."

"Right. But I've seen sparks between you two when I've been at the clinic with my Rufus." Mrs. Spencer waggled a forefinger, her eyes twinkling. "Great move on your part, I'd say, bidding at that auction. Anyway, I'm glad to have two vets in town in case Rufus gets sick again."

Darcy cast a wary glance around the toy-cluttered living room.

Rufus, with claws sharp as scalpels and teeth to match, was a disagreeable cat whether sick or well, and he had a memory like a five-gigabyte hard drive when it came to remembering the clinic staff who had dealt with him.

He also had a penchant for eating bizarre things like rubber bands and stretchy little hair ties left by the girls at the day care, which meant repeated trips to the clinic.

Mrs. Spencer followed her gaze. "Don't worry, dearie. I've started closing him upstairs when the kiddies are around so they can't play too rough with him."

Darcy suspected the rough behavior might be the other way around. "I know you must be really tired at the end of each day, but would you know of anyone who might be willing to babysit for an occasional Saturday night?"

"So I was right." She chortled. Her eyes gleamed in triumph. "It's always nice to help young sweethearts along."

Darcy couldn't help but roll her eyes. "You do know I could be talking about needing you for a church meeting at night. Or...or..."

"Well, whatever you're up to, I can always use a little pin money, so just give me a call. If I can't do it, you can always ask my niece. She might even come to your house."

On the way out to her car, Darcy tried to keep a firm grip on Emma's hand as the child skipped and hopped and then tried going backward. "What has gotten into you, sweetie? Are you this glad to go home?"

"Mrs. Spencer said you like Dr. Maxwell, so if you have a date then he can live with us. And then he could be my daddy 'cause I like him *lots*."

Darcy stifled a laugh as she tried to keep up with Emma's childish logic, though the potential for further embarrassment was obvious.

"Sounds like an interesting plan, sweetie—except things are never that easy. Keep it to yourself, okay? It would happen only if it was meant to be, and I doubt very much that it will."

After Emma had her bath, stories and bedtime snack, and finally fell asleep, Darcy worked into the night staining the kitchen floor to match what she'd done in the bedrooms.

As painstaking as the process was, it gave her way too much time to think.

She'd never thought a kiss could be so sweet. So

compelling. Logan's kiss had reverberated through her long afterward, and though once she might have dismissed her reaction as silly schoolgirl nonsense, even now she could feel the touch of his mouth on hers and the dizzying way he'd made her feel.

All with just a kiss.

Obviously she was way too susceptible and needed to get a grip. She had to make sure it didn't happen again.

After Dean, she'd been absolutely sure she never wanted to risk a relationship again. Nothing could possibly be worth the stress, the uncertainty. And from what Logan had once said, he felt exactly the same.

But what could have possibly gone badly enough in his life to make him that adamant?

He was intelligent, compassionate, dedicated, with good career. Handsome...and he was obviously great with kids, because Emma loved him. Just thinking about how sweet he'd been with old Mrs. Peabody and her dog still made Darcy feel warm inside. The list went on and on.

Then again, she'd blithely ignored the warning signs about Dean, and she'd learned that painful lesson all too well.

She'd be a fool to ignore Kaycee's muttered comment about something dark in Logan's past, and his sister's veiled reference about someone named Cathy. And what had Susan meant about a consuming anger that he'd never forgotten?

Out-of-control anger was something she never wanted to face again with any man. Ever.

The last swipe of the rag wet with stain took her to the kitchen door. Evening out that last swath of stain with the dry rag in her other hand, she surveyed the beautiful old hardwood that was now coming to life, then closed the can of stain and peeled off her gloves.

After a shower, she curled up on the couch with her laptop and pulled up Google. Thought long and hard about what she was about to do.

And then she typed in Logan's name.

Logan picked up his cell phone. Stared at it, then looked down at Cedar, who was sitting by his chair at the kitchen table. "So what do you think, old girl? Should I do this?"

The moth-eaten dog, now mostly covered in peach fuzz hair, laid her head on his thigh and looked up at him.

"Is that a yes? I could use some help here. Extend the invitation—yes or no?"

Cedar blinked.

He'd been on farm calls all morning and Darcy had worked at the clinic until noon, so he hadn't seen her since he'd kissed her last night. Even now he was second-guessing that move.

He'd never been so uncertain about a relationship in the past, through the few that had come and gone. He should have been far more uncertain about the last one and then avoided it all together.

But now, knowing about Darcy's past and her justified fear about involvement, he felt like he was traveling through unknown waters, as unsure as any teenage boy facing the terror of asking for his very first date.

What did he want here, really?

He wasn't even sure, except that being with Darcy and her little girl gave him a deep feeling of completion that had never been a part of his life. Whether he and Darcy were trading light banter or discussing vet cases, just talking to her made him smile. Made him want to be better, somehow. Made him long to be a part of a family. *Her* family.

And Emma...what a little pistol she was. Bright and talkative and curious, she made him laugh and made him want to protect her from anything that might ever dare try to harm her. He only had to look down at her to feel a sense of warmth settle in his heart.

Though after he'd impulsively kissed her mom last night, he might have thrown that all away.

He punched in Darcy's number, sat back in his chair and thanked God for church picnics and second chances.

"I didn't expect to be here today," Darcy said as she surveyed the shady city park. "What a perfect way to enjoy a Saturday afternoon."

Dozens of kids from the Sunday school classes were swinging, climbing on an old-fashioned jungle gym and lining up for the slides. Emma had already taken off at a run for her preschool friends, who were playing in a massive sandbox.

Darcy angled a look at Logan over the top rim of her sunglasses, then adjusted them into place. "How did you happen to find out about it?"

He shrugged. "There was a note about the Sunday school picnic in the church bulletin last weekend."

"It was nice of you to invite us. I'd forgotten about it, but this was good timing. I put down the first polyurethane coat on the kitchen floor this morning, and we needed to get out of the house. The fumes are really pungent." She frowned, looking at the long, food-laden tables in the picnic shelter. "I'll bet we were supposed to bring food. This is a potluck, right?

"Got it covered." He reached into a cooler in the back of his truck. "I bought a gallon of potato salad and a couple dozen M&M's cookies at the grocery store on my way to pick you up."

He handed her a blanket, and he carried the food as they strolled together through the sun-dappled shade of the massive oaks, nodding to the church families who had already spread out blankets or commandeered picnic tables. "Do you see a spot you'd like?"

"Up there on the knoll overlooking the playground."

She shook out the blanket in the deep shade beneath the massive branches of an oak while he took the food down to the buffet set up.

He brought back cups of icy lemonade. "They'll be having horseshoes, volleyball and also a softball game for the teenagers after lunch. Pastor Mark will say the prayer in a few minutes and then lunch will start. Are you glad you came?"

"It's a perfect day for this, and I'm so happy Emma's having a chance to play." She smiled softly, her gaze fixed on Emma and her little friends industriously digging in the sandbox. "Next year she'll start kindergarten, and I hear that once she starts school, she'll grow up in the blink of an eye. I feel like I have to savor every moment and memory before these years are gone."

She took a sip of lemonade. "I have to admit, I was a little surprised when you called about this."

"To tell you the truth, it's been a long time since I've had any part of being in a church family. If you'd told me six months ago that I'd ever be at a Sunday school picnic, I would've said you were crazy. But I'm honestly glad to be here. Especially with you and Emma."

"She adores you, you know." Darcy took another sip of her lemonade and flicked away an ant crawling across the blanket. "Probably too much. So I need to know something. Maybe this isn't the right time and place, but it really can't wait. I won't let her little heart be broken again by someone who disappoints her."

She fell silent for a moment, then looked across the picnic blanket and met his gaze. "I did a search of your name on Google last night. I suppose you already know why."

He knew what she was going to say. Back home, too many people already had. He stilled, quietly waiting for her to rail at him, then turn her back on him for good.

"I never would've thought to check, but your sister alluded to some trouble before you moved here. There were a lot of links to your name, but I couldn't bring myself to click any of them. It seemed wrong somehow. I'd rather that you told me yourself."

"And you'll believe me? I doubt it."

She fixed her piercing eyes on his. "I haven't known you long, but I've seen the kind of man you are. Tell me."

He didn't ever talk about his past—not with friends or family. Not with the counselor Susan had hired. Any words he managed to find did disservice to the depth of his grief and loss. None came close to truly honoring his late wife.

But he sensed that any chance to move on, any chance for a future, depended on getting this right. He took a slow breath and sent up a silent, rusty prayer.

"I was married in vet school," he said slowly. "Gina

was a year behind me. The sweetest, prettiest girl I'd ever met, and she totally stole my heart. We loved the same things—skiing, camping, high adventure stuff. I couldn't believe I'd found someone who loved all the things I did. We both wanted a big family and a horse farm in Montana, but we'd been married just two years when she died of stage IV breast cancer that showed up out of the blue. I was devastated beyond words."

"I am so, so sorry," Darcy said softly.

"Afterward, I joined a large vet practice and totally immersed myself in work. I was alone for five years. After losing Gina, I couldn't even look at another woman. Then one day, the group hired a new bookkeeper."

He looked away, and had to pause before he could continue. "I'd been wallowing in my grief since Gina died, but this gal was so sympathetic, so understanding and kind, that I fell into spending more and more time with her. She seemed like a lifeline to me, but she must have thought I was a sitting duck. Looking back, I'm not even sure when it happened or if it did. But suddenly she was happily announcing that we were engaged."

Darcy scanned the sandbox at the bottom of the hill, where Emma was building a sand castle. Then she looked back. "I'm almost afraid to hear the rest of this."

"Every expression of sympathy, every seemingly heartfelt emotion Cathy expressed was a ruse to mask her real intent. I was only a cover who unwittingly helped allay suspicions about her because, after all, she was with me, and I was a full partner. She embezzled around forty grand before being discovered, and then she disappeared. When they caught her, the money was gone—gambled away at casinos."

"So they got nothing back at all?"

He snorted. "In court she tried pinning it all on me. She said it was my idea, that I'd forced her into it. She said I'd kept the money myself and they needed to go after me instead. But the casino records and security videos showed otherwise. I don't gamble, and her attorney couldn't prove that I was ever in a casino with her."

"At least you were vindicated, then."

"Not entirely." He heaved a sigh. "The investigators found no proof against me, so I was never charged. Cathy went to prison a couple years ago. But the situation cast a veil of distrust over me as far as the other vets and clients were concerned. There are people who are still sure I helped her, pocketed the money or at least turned a blind eye. Even out on vet calls, I still got endless questions and innuendoes, and some clients questioned my character and professional skills. I finally gave up because it just wasn't worth it anymore. That's when I started looking for a practice somewhere in Minnesota or Wisconsin."

"What an awful situation to go through. I just can't imagine." She reached over to rest a hand on his forearm. "I wish I could have done something."

She already had, and she didn't know it. He'd arrived in Aspen Creek feeling betrayed and bitter, determined to keep his distance from anyone who tried to get too close. But she and her little girl had slipped beneath his defenses and reminded him of what good and decent people were like.

And now, he felt like he once again had a chance at a normal life. And if he could spend it with her, he would be well and truly blessed.

He rose to his feet and offered her a hand up. "Looks

like we ought to get down to the picnic shelter—most everyone has already gone through the line."

He started to step away from the blanket, but she caught his hand and tugged him back.

She looked up into his eyes. "I'm proud of you, Logan. For how you dealt with all of that, and for the man you are. Those people out West were so wrong about you. How could they not see it?"

This time, it was Darcy who started the kiss.

Lightly resting her hands on his chest, she raised up on her tiptoes to brush a kiss against his cheek. The wooded park, the sounds of adults talking and children playing and everything else in the world seemed to fade away, until it was only Darcy and him in this moment.

And when he gently pulled her into his arms for another kiss and she looked up at him again with those beautiful, luminous eyes, he felt like he was coming home.

Chapter Seventeen

The last week of May started unseasonably warm and muggy with rain most every day, but nothing could dampen Darcy's mood.

Tomorrow was the start of the three-day Memorial Day weekend. The clinic would be closed throughout, except for emergencies, and since she'd chosen Shaker-style kitchen cabinets that were available in the warehouse, they were already being delivered this afternoon.

Marilyn looked up from her computer screen. "I thought you were leaving at noon," she said with a smile. "Sounds like you have an exciting day."

"I'm on my way out now. And yes—you have no idea how thrilled I am to be almost done with the house. Just the cupboards, countertops and then some bathroom remodeling are left, and then everything will be done. For now, anyway."

Marilyn looked back at her screen. "It looks like Dr. Maxwell will be out on calls until four. Is he helping you tonight?"

"We're starting after supper, if all goes well."

"I guess you got a good deal at that auction in more

ways than one." Marilyn winked. "How is everything going with you two?"

Darcy shrugged, trying to contain her smile. "Pretty well, I think. We've been meeting at one house or the other for supper since the Sunday school picnic on Saturday. Emma is delighted because she gets to see the horses more often. And of course, she thinks Logan is her hero."

And, Darcy admitted only to herself, with each passing day she and Logan were becoming closer. Just the sound of his voice made her blood thrum in her veins, and every hour spent with him made her realize that she'd been truly blessed to find someone so wonderful.

It was way too soon to be thinking about a future together. But maybe, someday, if all went well...

"Just so you know, Kaycee and I will both be out of town this weekend. She's going to take her brother and sister to see relatives in Madison, and I'll be going to the Twin Cities with my husband."

"See you Tuesday, then. Travel safe." Darcy headed out the rear entryway and started to climb behind the wheel of her car.

"Wait!" Marilyn stood at the back door, waving frantically. "You need to see this."

Darcy followed her into the clinic. "What's up?"

Marilyn scurried down the hall ahead of her.

"It's on my computer screen. I...um, don't usually look at Facebook while I'm here." She gave an embarrassed little shrug. "But I was just starting to eat lunch at my desk. I happened to take a peek at my profile, and this came up in my feed. I don't know who this is—he calls himself the Aspen Creek Sentinel. His posts pop up now and then, usually about something around town, and he's often a little snide. A lot of locals comment on his posts. But *this*…"

Darcy leaned over to read the post. It had been shared from a newspaper website in Montana and included a photo of a beautiful young woman. The snippet of headline read Convicted of Fraud and Embezzlement, Woman Goes Free.

Darcy stared, her mouth suddenly dry. "Can you click on the link?"

"I already read it, and I printed it off. It's not good news. Did you know about this?"

Darcy felt her stomach twist into a cold knot. "I know she stole something like $40,000 from a vet clinic where Logan worked and tried to blame him. Why have they released her?"

"I don't understand all the mumbo-jumbo legal stuff, but it sounds like she's getting a retrial and has been released on bail." Marilyn reached over to grab some sheets of paper from the printer, stapled them and handed them to Darcy. "But the kicker is that she says she gave her lawyer new evidence that Logan was responsible in the first place—so he should have been tried, not her."

Darcy's stomach twisted even tighter. She closed her eyes in disbelief. "If that's true, he could be arrested and extradited back to Montana."

"*If* it's true?" Logan's voice came from behind her, the measured, emotionless tone cutting through her like a scalpel. "You apparently think it's a possibility?"

She whirled around to face his stony expression. "No—of course not. I meant if she or her lawyer come up with something, the court would have to check it out, and…" She faltered to a stop. "But surely she has falsified something, or flat-out lied. You said she was like that."

"All I know is that I had nothing to do with it. And whoever discovered this news must be standing on quite a soapbox around here." He cast a pointed glance at the papers in Darcy's hand. "Because three of my clients today had already heard about it, and one said he was taking his business elsewhere."

"That's so unfair. What are you going to do?"

"I've called my lawyer in Montana, and I'm going back. If Cathy has cooked up something plausible enough, there could be a long road ahead. And with the type of friends she probably made in prison, I don't even want to imagine it."

"What can I do? Just tell me," she pleaded.

"Nothing." He shrugged dismissively and turned away. "Nothing at all."

He'd known it was too good to be true—finding this idyllic little town, the kind of practice he'd dreamed of. Finding a woman and her little girl who had both touched his heart from the first time they'd met.

Well, maybe not the *first* time, he amended, remembering that first stony encounter at the clinic. But after that first meeting, things had warmed quickly, and he'd discovered such hope, such possibility, that maybe he would finally be on track toward the life he'd always wanted.

Then he'd heard that flicker of doubt in Darcy's voice and he'd pounced on it—seizing the chance to distance himself. No matter how much he cared for her, or how much he hoped she and little Emma could become his family someday, God willing, he knew what was coming, and she didn't deserve to be any part of it.

He'd already seen it happen.

The friendly greetings turned wary, the whispers of doubt among clients and people he barely knew. After all, some folks figured that shady lawyers could set free the most evil of men, so whether he was vindicated or not, there would be many who still thought another criminal had been freed.

And then the rumors would go on and on, expanding exponentially. Tainting the well that had once held only goodwill. And Darcy would suffer for it all only if she had any connection to him.

His first day here in town had been a case in point.

A client with an appointment in the clinic had overheard a misspoken statement. Offered it up to the local gossip mill.

So when Logan arrived at the café for an early lunch an hour later, the café clientele had turned on him as one, angry at his supposed mistreatment of one of their own.

Small in comparison to the catastrophe back in Montana, but awkward all the same.

He resolutely pushed open the door of the café, wondering if this visit would bring another charred hamburger and spilled beverage to his table. Prepared to ignore any comments and rebuffs, he found his usual front window booth and sat down without looking at the menu.

Marge, the morning waitress, came by with her pad and pencil. "The usual, Doc?"

He nodded, and she scurried off to the kitchen.

One by one, heads turned. Most of them silver or

gray and all of them familiar—mostly retired folk who could while away long hours over a shared slice of pie and coffee refills without regard for a time clock back at the job.

At the nearby round table, where a trio of older women usually reigned, all three heads turned. All of them frowned, and he braced himself.

"We wish you all the best, Doc," Mabel announced. "We read the news online and think it's abominable. It's clear enough that they ought to throw that tootsie back in jail."

The woman with the shortest silver hair nodded. "Just trying to get off the hook herself, I'd say. Some people would lie to their mothers if they thought it would do them any good."

The oldest woman—Mrs. Peabody—nodded. "We're all writing letters, you know. If that judge doesn't realize what a fine man you are, then he's going to find out. If you need character witnesses, we'll go to Montana."

That she would offer such a thing touched his heart. She barely had enough to live on as it was. "That's really kind of you all," he said, smiling at each lady in turn. "I appreciate it."

Wally, the old duffer with purple tennis shoes, came up to Logan's booth and pounded a fist on the table. "We've seen how good you are to Doc Leighton and her little girl, and we've seen you around town. You're good folks. If things go south, we'll take up a collection. Mark my words."

Logan hated to think what even a few dollars meant to some of these people. "Thank you, Wally. But I don't think things will come to that."

"If they do, we'll send you news from home. You can have mail in prison, right?"

Mrs. Peabody gasped. "Wally, no one is going anywhere. He'll get things straightened out, because he's innocent."

Beth had told him about the community spirit here when he'd first arrived. How folks banded together to help their own, and stood by their friends.

So how ironic it was, to learn that he'd become a part of that kinship when he might soon have to leave?

Darcy eyed the mountain of cardboard boxes stacked in her kitchen and sighed.

She'd been excited about this delivery and the chance to help Logan install the new cabinets today. With Emma safely out of the way at Mrs. Spencer's, they could've gotten so much done.

And she'd been so happy about the long weekend ahead, because she and Logan had planned be together every day.

She'd lined up Mrs. Spencer's niece to babysit several times over the long weekend, so if the stormy weather forecast cleared, she and Logan had planned to rent kayaks to explore the St. Croix, and later on take his horses on a long trail ride.

They were also going to take Emma along for cookouts at the park and take her wading at the beach. Simple things. The kind of family times that she always recorded with lots of iPhone photos so she could create photo books, and Emma could see glimpses of her happy childhood after she'd grown.

But now Darcy had seen Logan angrily blow her comment about his legal situation all out of proportion, and he wasn't answering his phone or responding to texts. How could he have become so volatile over a single misconstrued comment when everything had been going so well? How could he not be willing to discuss it and work things out?

It didn't make sense.

And it made her worry.

Had this relationship been heading toward the boundaries that she'd sworn she'd never cross? A deeper commitment that could lead to heartbreak?

Dean had changed over the years. He'd become defensive and petulant, and his anger had grown way out of control the year before he finally walked out on her.

Darcy had done her best to shield Emma from their verbal battles, but on that last night her little girl had awakened and come out into the living room at just the wrong time. Seeing her pale and frightened face had been the final, defining moment.

Whatever Darcy's beliefs about marriage and forgiveness and trying to make things work, raising Emma in a safe, loving home, with a good example of how men should treat their families, mattered most of all. She would have left with Emma the next morning if Dean hadn't already gone.

Now she could look back and see that his unconscionable outbursts likely correlated to times when he was totally enamored with some other woman. He'd probably been consumed with frustration and anger over the complexities of being a cheat—while still inconveniently involved in a business with his wife.

Maybe he'd even felt a little guilt, if Darcy wanted to give him that much benefit of the doubt.

But no good and decent father put his selfish desires

above the welfare of his daughter and the bounds of marriage. And no man—no matter how appealing— would ever have a place in Darcy's heart if he had Dean's dark and angry side.

Ever.

And that brought her back to Logan.

She wandered through the house, adjusting the tilt of Aunt Tina's artwork on the walls. Running her hand over the furnishings she'd arranged in the living room and bedrooms now that the beautiful old floors glowed with burnished charm.

Despite what Logan thought he'd heard her say, she did trust him to be honorable in all things, because she seen him with clients, Emma and the staff.

Even when he hadn't realized that others could inadvertently overhear him, his kindness had never wavered. He'd erased more than one bill for an elderly client on welfare and examined a child's puppy when there was no way the family could pay. And that was just when she'd been around to notice.

There was no way Logan Maxwell would have embezzled that money in Montana. No way at all.

But unprovoked anger…that was another issue entirely. One she would never tolerate. Should she call him on it? Make herself perfectly clear on that score?

Apparently it was a moot point, if they were no longer speaking.

With a sigh, she grabbed her keys and purse to go after Emma, who would be far better company than an irritable Montana cowboy who apparently didn't know what he was throwing away.

But if she managed to track Logan Maxwell down, she would definitely be letting him know.

Chapter Eighteen

Storms rolled through late Friday night, and Saturday morning was unseasonably hot and muggy. By afternoon the humidity was ninety percent and felt like wearing a blanket in a sauna.

With the clinic closed for the long weekend and both Marilyn and Kaycee out of town, there was no one to ask about any calls from Logan, and there were no calls on the office answering machine when Darcy stopped in to check on the two canine patients that had needed to stay over the holiday.

The kennel girl always came early to clean cages and feed any animals before going to her next job, so Darcy had rarely seen her, but everything was clean and in perfect order back in the kennels.

Coming back down the hall, she paused at the door of Logan's office. There was no sign that he'd been here today—the desk was tidied, with no half-empty coffee cups or the scattered papers of a task in progress. The computer was off.

She started to call his cell, then dropped the phone back into her purse.

If he glanced at his incoming calls, he'd see that she'd tried several times already. Many more tries and she would seem like an obsessive, scorned woman bent on confrontation.

If he had any desire to talk, he knew her number.

The stormy sky was darkening as she drove home with Emma after stops at the grocery store and the old-fashioned ice cream store for a hamburger and a sundae.

But it was the sudden sickly green tint overhead and the deadly calm air that had her worried.

"Can we go to the park?" Emma craned her neck to look around and pointed. "We could go that way."

Darcy glanced at the rearview mirror. "I'd like to, sweetie. But we have groceries that need to be in the fridge, and it looks like rain. Maybe we can go after supper."

"Please?"

"Later." Darcy pulled to a stop at the next corner and turned right.

The flowers at the base of the stop sign were as still as a watercolor painting, ominous for all their beauty. The leaves on the trees were motionless.

The birds were silent.

Darcy flipped through the radio channels as she drove the last few blocks to their house, catching only snatches of music and talk shows.

No one on the radio seemed concerned. It was probably nothing. Maybe just a front blowing through.

But as she drove slowly up Cranberry Lane, past the stately brick homes that overshadowed her own little cottage, she began to see curtains pulled back to reveal worried faces and a few of the neighbors standing outside with hands on their hips, staring up at the sky.

At home, she drove into the garage, grabbed the groceries and Emma and hurried into the house, clicking the garage door closed with the remote on her key ring. Even here, the towering oaks were motionless.

Lightning cracked in the distance, followed by a long roll of thunder.

Bonnie scrabbled at the back door as Darcy unlocked it. She raced outside, then threw herself at the door to come back in.

As soon as the door reopened, she came in with her tail tucked and pressed herself against Darcy's leg.

Emma wrapped her arms round the dog. "I'm scared, Mommy. Bonnie is, too."

"It's okay—I promise. We've got a nice, safe basement, so we can go down there if the weather gets worse, and there haven't been any sirens going off, so—"

A low, piercing siren split the air, rising to an ear-splitting high note, then slowly undulating. Another siren began in some other part of town, and the discordant wails sent a shiver down Darcy's spine.

"That's our cue, sweetheart. Let's go." On her way to the stairs, Darcy shoved her cell phone in her pocket, then grabbed her purse, a flashlight and the old-fashioned portable radio Aunt Tina had always kept on top of the fridge. She took Emma's hand and descended the steep, narrow wooden stairs with Bonnie close at her heels.

At the bottom, she pulled the cord dangling in front of her to turn on a single bank of fluorescent lights over the washer and dryer.

Emma trembled. "I don't like it down here, Mommy. It's scary."

It wasn't a place Darcy enjoyed much, either. The

house had been built in the 1900s and no doubt re-modeled many times, but the four basement walls were original—constructed of massive, uneven stones held together with cement, and the floor was perpetually damp.

As a child she'd thought it reminiscent of a dungeon in some spooky, medieval castle, but during the intervening years, Aunt Tina had painted the walls a stark white. It was less gloomy now, though the lights still threw dark shadows in the corners where anything in a little girl's imagination might hide.

Darcy squeezed Emma's hand and smiled. "Do you know what? Even with a dehumidifier, it's too damp down here ever to finish off as a family room, but I think I'll put another coat of white on the walls and have a lot more lights installed. At least it will be nicer if we have to come down here again during a storm."

Emma wrapped her arms around Bonnie's neck. "Can we go back upstairs yet?"

Rain and hail battered at the narrow basement windows. Lightning flashed and thunder roared and a loud *crack!* shook the house, sending dust swirling down from the floor joists above their heads.

At the far side, cement steps led up to the sloped cellar doors leading to the backyard. They'd been padlocked for as long as Darcy remembered, and she'd never tried to open them, but now they rattled and bucked against the high winds, the hinges squealing.

Logan.

His name slammed into her thoughts. A warning, a plea. Where was he? What if he hadn't answered his phone because he was lying somewhere hurt, unable to call?

Or maybe he'd already been arrested and extradited back to Montana—though she had no idea if such things could happen that fast.

Thinking about his sharp comment and remembering Dean's temper, she'd assumed the worst about his behavior. She hadn't tried calling again.

She felt her heart wrench.

If something bad had happened, she hadn't had a chance to say goodbye. Then again, maybe it was just this weather giving her such dark thoughts.

Now the screaming of the warning sirens competed with the strident wailing of emergency vehicles, and Darcy's heart pounded.

Ten minutes later, silence fell.

Emma hugged her dog tighter and looked up, her eyes round and frightened. "Is our house okay, Mommy?"

"I think so. Just take my hand while we go up."

Darcy slowly made her way up the stairs and opened the door into the kitchen.

The sky was starting to lighten, but the wind still sent buffets of rain against the windows. She walked through the house, checking the windows for damage and surveying the yard, with Emma and Bonnie close at her heels.

"The house seems fine, but I'll need to stand outside to see if we lost any shingles. Look here—out the front window."

A massive oak lay uprooted in the neighbor's yard, blocking his drive and most of the street. One branch had broken away the front porch.

Power lines lay in tangles on the street beneath its upper branches and were sparking and snapping between the neighbor's house and the next one down.

"They won't be going anywhere soon." Darcy flicked a light switch. Sure enough, the power was out. "But our drive is clear, and none of the power lines are compromised at the other end of the block, so I believe we can get out safely. I'm going to try."

Emma's eyes filled with worry. "Where are we going?"

"I need to check on Logan, so you get to play with Mrs. Spencer for an hour or so. I just don't want…" Darcy hesitated. "I just want you to have some fun for a while. It'll be really boring if you come with me."

The rain slowed, then stopped. She glanced at her cell phone again. No calls, no texts. But of course not—she would have heard the alert.

She called 911 for police assistance to check on the neighbors, and the power company to report the downed wires.

Biting her lower lip, she tried calling Logan again. No answer. Then she dialed Mrs. Spencer.

If Logan no longer cared about her, so be it.

But she had to make sure he wasn't lying injured somewhere at his place and in need of help. And if he was, she couldn't waste another minute. *Please, Lord, let him be all right.*

Chapter Nineteen

The streets were clear to Mrs. Spencer's house, though after Darcy dropped off Emma and headed out of town, she encountered numerous uprooted trees and heavy branches blocking the streets.

After zigzagging through town to avoid the blockages and power company utility vehicles, she finally made it onto the county road leading out to Logan's. The damage was even greater out here, cutting a swath heading to the northeast through the heavy timber.

At the lane leading up to his place, she repeatedly had to get out of her car to drag heavy branches to one side. Up around the house and barn, the damage was worse.

Several large pines had toppled over in his yard, and one had broken through the fence. Another one had landed on roof of his house at a crazy angle, and it looked as if some of the branches had crashed through the shingles and into the attic.

"Logan?" She ran toward the barn, calling his name, then surveyed the corrals. Not even the horses were in sight, though when a whinny echoed from the barn, she found just the bay gelding in a box stall. At the house, she jerked open the front door and ran through the rooms, searching for him to no avail.

His truck was still in the garage. But it didn't appear that he'd left for Montana on his own volition or otherwise.

His billfold and truck keys lay on the kitchen counter. A plate on the counter held a raw steak, ready to grill. Where in the world was he? And where was his dog?

Every doubt she'd had about him, every nonchalant thought about easily walking away from him after that last tumultuous encounter, all dissolved, leaving her feeling bruised and empty.

She didn't need explanations or apologies or even promises…she just needed to find him and make sure he was all right. Nothing else mattered.

Because Logan Maxwell had truly stolen her heart.

Exhausted, Logan rubbed his free hand over Drifter's muddy neck and continued the litany of reassurances that he no longer believed.

State forest backed up to his secluded place on three sides, his driveway was long, and traffic was rare on the county road passing his property.

If not for the rusty mailbox, a stranger driving past wouldn't even know his place existed, much less think to traverse his twenty acres of timber and meadow unless hunting illegally. And without any phone reception out here in this hilly terrain, there was no way to call for help.

So he was here alone, except for his injured horse and a dog that kept running off. He would hear Cedar barking her head off somewhere, and then she'd come back, even during the worst of the storm today. If she was hunting, she hadn't brought back any evidence of prey, but she'd looked more weary with every trip into the forest.

If he even moved a few feet, his beloved Drifter would bleed out. So he'd stood beside her to compress her wound and keep her still, and tried to keep the sharp branch impaled in her chest from moving. The miracle was that it hadn't severed a major artery...yet.

There was nothing else he could do unless some-one happened by—as improbable as seeing a penguin toddle past—except for mulling over the stupid things he'd done in his lifetime and wishing he had another chance to do them right.

And he could pray.

Since last night he'd had plenty of time for that.

He'd started out angry at God last night for taunting him with the inevitable loss of his beloved mare, right after he'd walked out on the best thing in his life. *Darcy.*

Though he still counted himself a believer, for years his rebellious heart had refused the thought of prayer in a time of need. Why bother? His prayers had sure never been answered before when it mattered most.

He'd prayed relentlessly, tearfully, as a teenager when Dad had his heart attack and died. Had prayed desper-ately when Mom died months afterward. And during the long months of Gina's illness, he'd begged God to save her.

None of his prayers had saved the people he loved.

But today he'd stood out in the forest through a fierce storm, with lightning crashing all around him, refusing to give up on Drifter's life. And in his exhaustion and desperation during those interminable hours, the words of his family's pastor nudged at him, prodded at the wall of ice around his heart. *God created this world and the laws of nature that exist. He doesn't want terrible things to happen...he doesn't cause them, Logan. But when they strike, he wants to surround us with his loving arms and give us strength, and hope, and peace. And the people around you are an answer to your prayers.*

As the hours passed, he finally began to understand how wrong he'd been about those prayers. God had answered in other ways. The wonderful, supportive hospice staff. The friends and family who had hovered like angels to offer loving comfort. Who had stepped up to help with the harvest, the cattle, the horses, and helped Susan and him deal with the deluge of decisions that followed.

From far away came the sound of Cedar barking. Barking. Barking. Slowly coming closer. But it was a different sound this time—more agitated.

If she was after a badger or other fierce wild prey, there wouldn't be a thing he could do to help her. *Please, Lord, bring someone to help me...and please keep that foolish dog safe.*

She fell silent. Then he heard her crashing through the brush close by.

And this time, there were footsteps behind her.

If she hadn't heard Cedar's frantic barking, Darcy never would've known which way to go. She pulled to a halt the moment she saw Logan and his mare.

Drifter was caught in a tangle of downed pine trees, with an undoubtedly sharp broken branch protruding from her chest.

Pale, clearly exhausted and weaving on his feet,

Logan was holding that branch steady and stemming the flow of blood from a wound on her neck that might well have sliced an artery, given its position.

She instantly assessed the situation. "One of us needs to stay. The other needs to bring back the right equipment—stat. Tell me what you want me to do."

"I need to stay and keep her stable."

Darcy had never run so fast in her life, through the brush. Picking up random deer trails. Praying. She made it to the clinic and back in under an hour, laden with everything she could carry that they might need.

After delivering an intravenous sedative, she spread a sterile surgical drape on the ground and laid out her instruments, surgical gloves and a bag of sterile saline for flushing the wounds. "You or me?"

"It had better be you. I'm not sure I could even hang on to a scalpel right now."

Within an hour she'd meticulously cleaned the wounds. Repaired the neck injury.

Sutured the inner layers of the gaping chest wound, and sutured what she could of the outer layer. After delivering an intramuscular dose of long-acting antibiotic, she gathered up her equipment and rolled it up into the surgical drape.

"It's the best I can do out here without better light," she said, giving Logan a closer look. He was muddy and streaked with blood. Given the gash on one cheekbone, some of that blood was his own. His shirt was torn, and from what she could tell, he was barely staying on his feet. "You look awful. Why don't you start home? When Drifter is more alert, I can lead her back to the barn."

"I'll wait."

"No, you should go. There's no way I can carry you

home if you collapse, and I doubt the EMTs could get here anytime soon. They probably have their hands full with all that happened in town."

"How bad was it?"

"I saw a lot of trees down, some damaged roofs. But I just saw a part of town on my way out here, so I don't know about the other areas. There were a lot of sirens."

"Your house okay?"

"Good. But yours didn't fare quite as well. There's a tree down on your roof, and another one broke your fence line."

He nodded. "That corral fence went down in the storm last night. Charlie was easy to catch, so I put him in the barn, but Drifter was still racing around in the yard. I opened the pasture gate in case she headed that way. Figured I could get her into the barn that way, but lightning struck close by and she just kept running until she crashed into this."

"Why didn't you call me? I would've come right away."

"I figured helping me would be the last thing on your mind. A little later on I came to my senses and figured at least you might send someone else, but then I realized that there's no reception out here. If I left her, she might've bled to death."

Darcy wanted to shake him. "You angrily misconstrued what I said to Marilyn at the clinic. You gave me no chance to explain, and then you walked away. But I certainly would have helped you anyway. That's what friends do. But just so you know, Dean acted like that all the time, and I'll never, ever go through that again. Not with anyone. So—"

She faltered to a stop and took another hard look at him. His gaze veered away.

"Wait. You did that on purpose?"

He didn't answer.

"Why?" She thought back over the last few weeks. Despite her resolution not to become romantically involved with anyone after her disastrous marriage, she'd thought she and Logan were becoming closer. She'd even kissed him. Twice. But clearly he hadn't shared her feelings. He'd been trying to get rid of her, for goodness' sake. Embarrassment burned through her. "Never mind. I can guess."

"Look, you've built a good life for yourself. You don't deserve to be mixed up in my problems," he said wearily. "You have no idea what it's like. The rumors. The doubts. Even after you're proven innocent, people figure you're guilty and just got off easy. It's why I finally left my last practice. And now, apparently it has caught up with me here."

So this wasn't about a brush-off, then. He'd been trying to *protect* her? In a completely awkward and somehow endearing way, but still.

"Look. I'm sorry that your ex-girlfriend is trying to stir up trouble. I'm sorry that you might need to go back to Montana to prove her wrong and get this straightened out. But I know from the bottom of my heart that you're totally innocent. I know what kind of man you are, and none of that stuff in Montana matters. I just hope it can be straightened out for good, so you'll never have to deal with it again."

A faint smile crooked one side of his mouth. "I have it on good authority that the morning crowd at the cafe all want to be my character witnesses. One old duffer even offered to take up a collection for my defense."

"That would be Wally. Purple shoes?"

"Yep—and he also promised to send me prison mail if things don't work out."

She laughed. "After a slow start with the locals, it sounds like you've won them over, after all. Just think. You've got an excellent staff at your clinic. A devoted following in the over-eighty crowd, and a dog smart enough to go for help. She came and got me, you know. I was headed the wrong away and she kept barking and trying to lead me here."

Drifter's ears flickered. She raised her head a few inches as she started to coming out of the sedation. Logan stroked her neck. "About the future…"

She felt her heart still.

"I've talked to my banker and my lawyer about drawing up an offer for a contract, with annual payments leading to full partnership. Just what Dr. Boyd planned, if you're still interested."

It was what she'd hoped for. The perfect resolution. Starting a practice of her own would have involved a huge investment and a great deal of risk.

Yet…it took some effort to smile.

Was that all there was between them—just a business contract? Had she been wrong all along about where this might be going?

One day she'd be locked into a full partnership—granted, in a career she loved—and when he found a beautiful bride and had two beautiful children, she'd get to stand by for the rest of her career and see them all have a beautiful life.

The thought was depressing.

He'd moved a little closer while she was thinking those cheery thoughts, and now he rested a hand on her shoulder and gently lifted her chin with his other forefinger. "I thought you'd be happy. Isn't this what you wanted all along?"

"Yes—yes, of course."

"If you'd rather just be an associate, that's fine, too. But I thought you'd rather have a legal stake in the business, come what may. It would give you more financial security."

"Absolutely. Thanks." She looked away, not quite able to meet his eyes, knowing he would see only disappointment, not satisfaction. *Legal* stake? This was only *business*?

Then she lifted her gaze to his.

The warmth in his eyes sent a shiver straight to her toes.

"I know it's early days, but—" his voice roughened "—I love you, Darcy. If we can only be partners, so be it. But if you say there's even a chance for us, you'll make me the happiest guy in Aspen Creek."

She reached up on tiptoes and pulled him down for a kiss that answered his question and more. And when he drew her into an embrace, she melted against him, wrapped her arms around his neck and kissed him again.

And looked forward to what the future might bring.

Epilogue

Logan slipped an arm around Darcy's waist and leaned over to kiss her cheek, then picked up Emma as the bridal party gathered under the trees. "You two look beautiful tonight, ladies."

Darcy grinned up at him. "Mighty good-looking yourself, cowboy. You clean up exceptionally well."

The old phrase was certainly appropriate—not two hours ago, they'd been performing an operation on a severe colic case, and they'd made it out here to the county park with minutes to spare. Now, Logan was wearing a dark sports jacket and gray slacks, while Emma wore a flouncy, fluffy dress with matching pink socks and shoes.

Darcy had resisted buying a dress for herself, then found a silver sheath dress with matching shoes at the last minute.

They slipped into the back row of chairs, where Emma wouldn't be a distraction if she got restless. "Can I stay up for fireworks, Mommy?"

Darcy doubted she'd last that long, but smiled. "You can sure give it a try."

The small crowd was settling into the white chairs facing a simple altar set up along the shore of Aspen Creek. Off to one side, the harpist finished playing the beautifully haunting strains of "Somewhere in Time." Then the violinist seated next to her joined in a duet of "Ave Maria." The sweet, achingly emotional violin sent shivers through Darcy, and she closed her eyes to savor every note.

"This couldn't be a more perfect evening or a more beautiful wedding," she whispered. "I'm just so happy for Hannah and Ethan."

The harpist began a solo of Canon in D by Pachelbel. Everyone rose and turned as the wedding party came down the aisle—Molly and Cole, the niece and nephew whom Hannah had adopted, and their two dogs, each sporting a big white bow.

"I hear Ethan's paperwork is completed, so he will be adopting the kids, as well," Darcy whispered. "Hannah says he's thrilled about making it official."

Hannah and Ethan walked down the grassy aisle next, arm in arm, to join the children. Hannah's radiant expression and Ethan's adoration of her touched Darcy's heart.

Throughout the open-air chapel, she saw other friends and neighbors and people from church, and her heart warmed. Coming to this town after closing a painful chapter in her life had been one of the best decisions she'd ever made and had led her to the most wonderful man she could have imagined.

She smiled to herself, remembering that first day when she found an unexpected stranger in the clinic and thought he spelled disaster for her future in Aspen

Creek. And later, when she'd gone to auction and ended up losing Edgar but gaining the best prize of all. Surely God's hand had been guiding her, because otherwise she might never have ended up so blessed.

After the wedding buffet, some of the guests left, but the rest settled on a hill in the park to watch the fireworks display. Emma curled up in Logan's lap, her eyes already closing as the dazzling explosions of diamonds filled the sky.

Logan looked down at her with chagrin. "I hope you'll both remember this as a really special day, so I got each of you something. But I'm afraid she won't be awake to see hers until tomorrow."

"What is it? Can you tell me?"

He took another look at Emma's sleeping face, then lowered his voice to a whisper. "I hope she'll be happy to find that her preschool pal isn't the only little girl with a playhouse."

"She will love it! Thank you so much!"

He grinned. "That's not all. Remember Pepper?"

"Anna's pony. Oh, no—did her dad make her give him up?"

"He stopped by this morning." He looked down at Emma to see if she was still asleep, then continued in a lower voice. "Anna's riding instructor found them a pony a little better suited for her. He said he wanted a good home for Pepper and has given him to Emma as a gift."

"That's wonderful," Darcy breathed. "Emma will be so thrilled."

Logan slipped something from his pocket and handed it to her, then draped an arm around her shoulders and drew her close. "And here is something for you. Not quite as big as a pony, unfortunately."

Her heart stilled as she stared at the small box in his hand.

"You can open it later if you want, but this just seemed like the perfect place to give it to you."

She turned the small box over, savoring the moment. Wondering if she was holding the key to her entire future in the palm of her hand. Slowly, very slowly, she lifted the lid, barely able to breathe.

Inside lay a platinum engagement band strewn with diamonds, with a glittering solitaire at its center. "Oh, it's…it's stunning!"

He gave he shoulders a little squeeze. "Try it on and see if it fits."

She slid it on her ring finger, feeling utterly dazzled. So happy she could barely contain her emotions.

His eyes twinkled. "So what do you say, Darcy Leighton? Same date next year?"

Mindful of her sleeping daughter, she turned to cradle his beloved face with her hands and leaned closer to draw him into a kiss.

The biggest and brightest of the fireworks were now filling the sky, but they didn't begin to match what she felt, with Logan in her arms.

* * * * *

Dear Reader,

Thank you so much for joining me in Aspen Creek once again! I've loved writing about this small town set in the beautiful river bluff country of western Wisconsin.

This book in the Aspen Creek Crossroads series was great fun to write, because I love small towns, country life and animals. My husband and I live in just such a place—an acreage out in the country with our three horses, two beloved dogs we adopted from an animal shelter, and five exceptionally friendly cats who like to wind around my ankles when I head down to the barn to do horse chores.

If you've enjoyed this book, you might want to find the previous Aspen Creek Crossroads novels: *Winter Reunion, Second Chance Dad, An Aspen Creek Christmas*, and *A Single Dad's Redemption*, which can be found at Harlequin.com or on Amazon.

I love to hear from readers and can be contacted by snailmail at PO Box 2550, Cedar Rapids, Iowa 52401, or online at www.roxannerustand.com, www.facebook.com/Roxanne.Rustand, www.SweetRomanceReads.com, and www.pinterest.com/roxannerustand.

Wishing you abundant blessings,

Roxanne